GOSCINNY AND UDERZO
PRESENT
An Asterix Adventure

ASTERIX
AND
CAESAR'S GIFT

Written by RENÉ GOSCINNY *and Illustrated by* ALBERT UDERZO

Translated by Anthea Bell *and* Derek Hockridge

Asterix titles available now

© 1974 GOSCINNY/UDERZO
Revised edition and English translation © 2004 HACHETTE
Original title: *Le Cadeau de César*

Exclusive licensee: Orion Publishing Group
Translators: Anthea Bell and Derek Hockridge
Typography: Bryony Newhouse

This revised edition first published in 2004 by Orion Books Ltd,
Orion House, 5 Upper Saint Martin's Lane, London WC2H 9EA
An Hachette UK company

9 10 8

Printed in China

www.asterix.com/english/
www.orionbooks.co.uk

A CIP record for this book is available from the British Library

ISBN-13 978-0-7528-6645-1 (cased)
ISBN-13 978-0-7528-6646-8 (paperback)

Distributed in the United States of America by Sterling Publishing Co. Inc.
387 Park Avenue South, New York, NY 10016

The Orion Publishing Group's policy is to use papers that are natural, renewable and recyclable products
and made from wood grown in sustainable forests. The logging and manufacturing processes are
expected to conform to the environmental regulations of the country of origin.

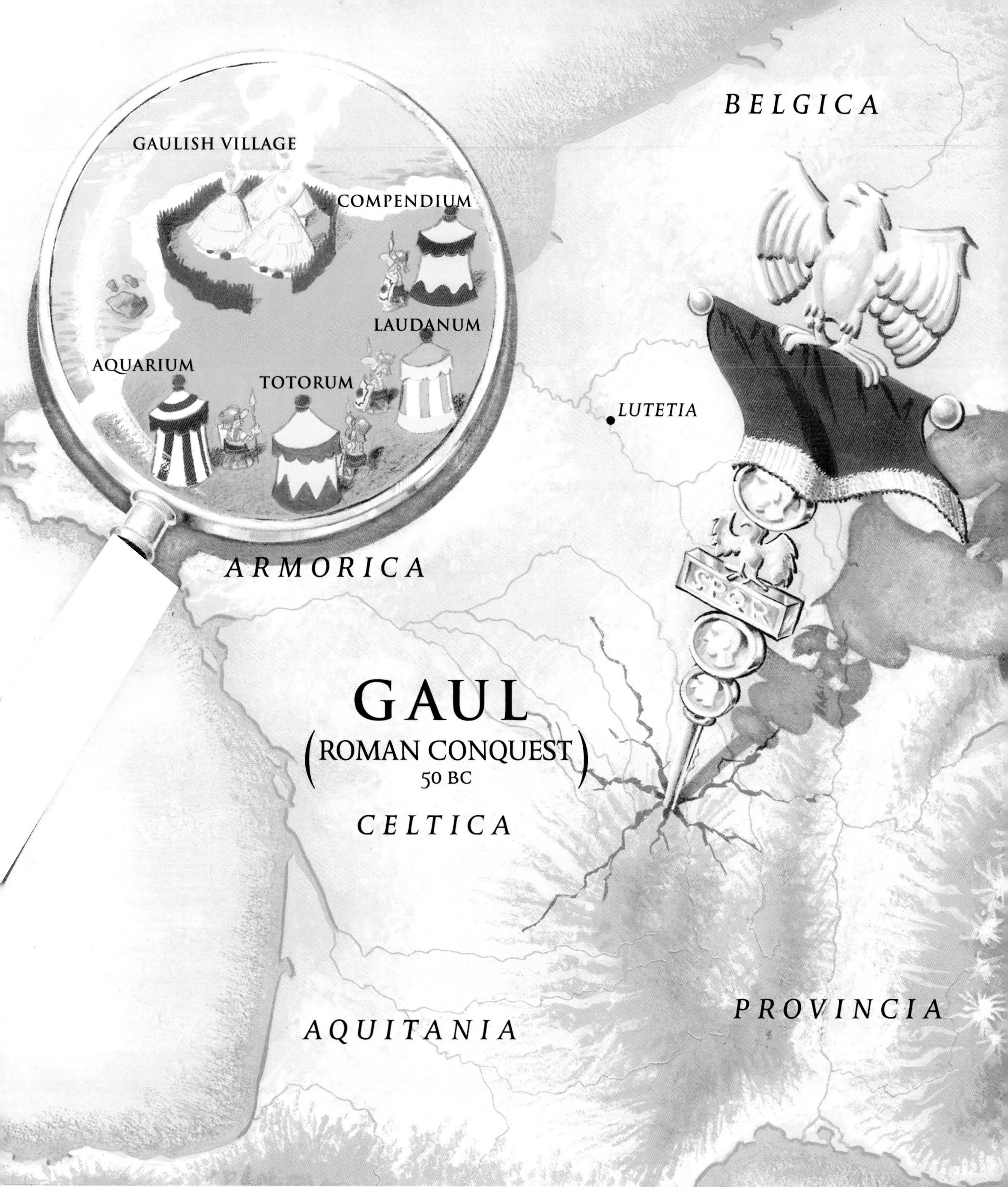
BELGICA
GAULISH VILLAGE
COMPENDIUM
LAUDANUM
AQUARIUM
TOTORUM
LUTETIA
SPQR
ARMORICA
GAUL
(ROMAN CONQUEST)
50 BC
CELTICA
PROVINCIA
AQUITANIA

THE YEAR IS 50 BC. GAUL IS ENTIRELY OCCUPIED BY THE ROMANS. WELL, NOT ENTIRELY … ONE SMALL VILLAGE OF INDOMITABLE GAULS STILL HOLDS OUT AGAINST THE INVADERS. AND LIFE IS NOT EASY FOR THE ROMAN LEGIONARIES WHO GARRISON THE FORTIFIED CAMPS OF TOTORUM, AQUARIUM, LAUDANUM AND COMPENDIUM …

ASTERIX, THE HERO OF THESE ADVENTURES. A SHREWD, CUNNING LITTLE WARRIOR, ALL PERILOUS MISSIONS ARE IMMEDIATELY ENTRUSTED TO HIM. ASTERIX GETS HIS SUPERHUMAN STRENGTH FROM THE MAGIC POTION BREWED BY THE DRUID GETAFIX . . .

OBELIX, ASTERIX'S INSEPARABLE FRIEND. A MENHIR DELIVERY MAN BY TRADE, ADDICTED TO WILD BOAR. OBELIX IS ALWAYS READY TO DROP EVERYTHING AND GO OFF ON A NEW ADVENTURE WITH ASTERIX – SO LONG AS THERE'S WILD BOAR TO EAT, AND PLENTY OF FIGHTING. HIS CONSTANT COMPANION IS DOGMATIX, THE ONLY KNOWN CANINE ECOLOGIST, WHO HOWLS WITH DESPAIR WHEN A TREE IS CUT DOWN.

GETAFIX, THE VENERABLE VILLAGE DRUID, GATHERS MISTLETOE AND BREWS MAGIC POTIONS. HIS SPECIALITY IS THE POTION WHICH GIVES THE DRINKER SUPERHUMAN STRENGTH. BUT GETAFIX ALSO HAS OTHER RECIPES UP HIS SLEEVE . . .

CACOFONIX, THE BARD. OPINION IS DIVIDED AS TO HIS MUSICAL GIFTS. CACOFONIX THINKS HE'S A GENIUS. EVERY-ONE ELSE THINKS HE'S UNSPEAKABLE. BUT SO LONG AS HE DOESN'T SPEAK, LET ALONE SING, EVERYBODY LIKES HIM . . .

FINALLY, VITALSTATISTIX, THE CHIEF OF THE TRIBE. MAJESTIC, BRAVE AND HOT-TEMPERED, THE OLD WARRIOR IS RESPECTED BY HIS MEN AND FEARED BY HIS ENEMIES. VITALSTATISTIX HIMSELF HAS ONLY ONE FEAR, HE IS AFRAID THE SKY MAY FALL ON HIS HEAD TOMORROW. BUT AS HE ALWAYS SAYS, TOMORROW NEVER COMES.

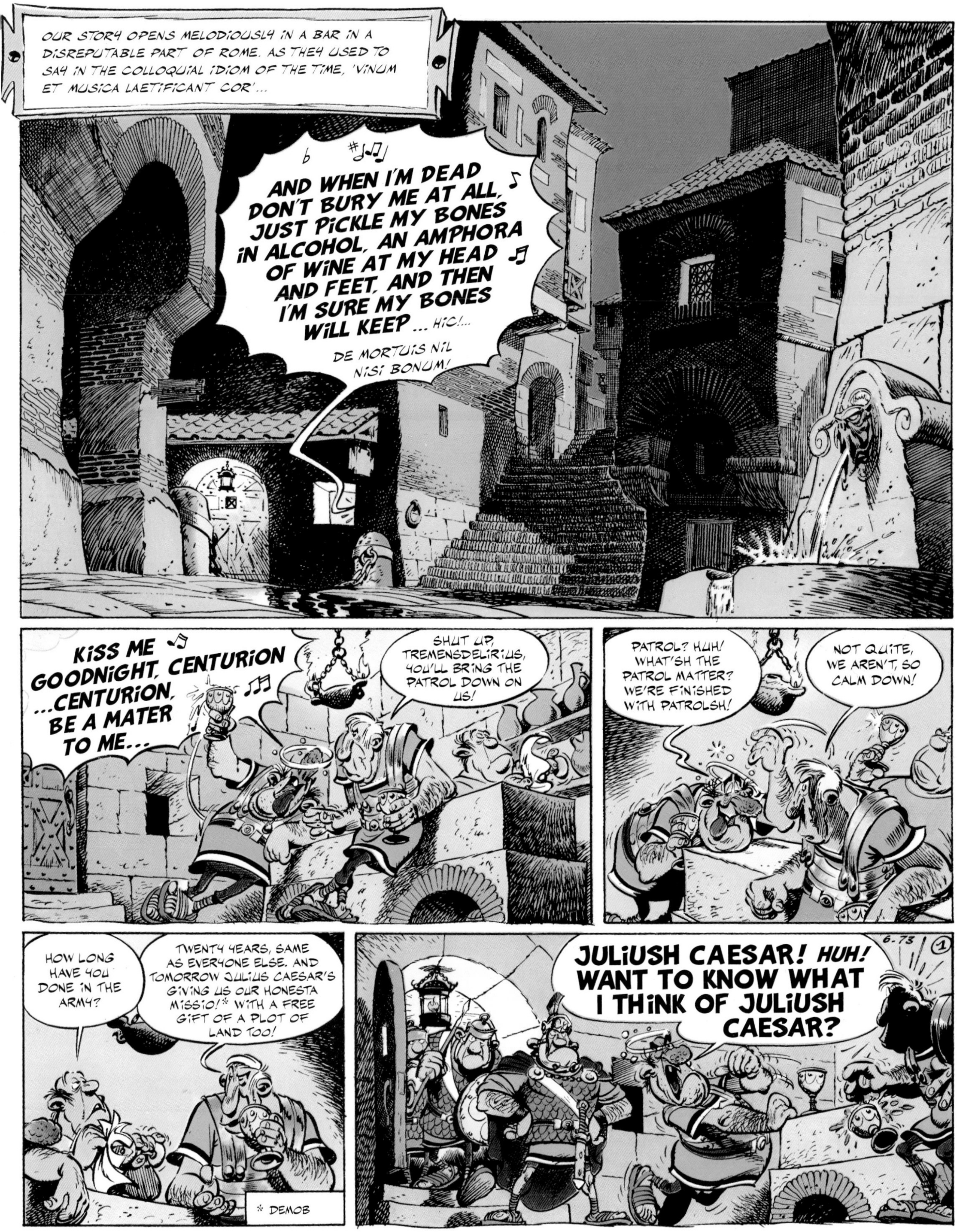

OUR STORY OPENS MELODIOUSLY IN A BAR IN A DISREPUTABLE PART OF ROME. AS THEY USED TO SAY IN THE COLLOQUIAL IDIOM OF THE TIME, 'VINUM ET MUSICA LAETIFICANT COR'...
AND WHEN I'M DEAD DON'T BURY ME AT ALL, JUST PICKLE MY BONES IN ALCOHOL, AN AMPHORA OF WINE AT MY HEAD AND FEET, AND THEN I'M SURE MY BONES WILL KEEP ... HIC!...
DE MORTUIS NIL NISI BONUM!
KISS ME GOODNIGHT, CENTURION ...CENTURION, BE A MATER TO ME...
SHUT UP, TREMENSDELIRIUS, YOU'LL BRING THE PATROL DOWN ON US!
PATROL? HUH! WHAT'SH THE PATROL MATTER? WE'RE FINISHED WITH PATROLSH!
NOT QUITE, WE AREN'T, SO CALM DOWN!
HOW LONG HAVE YOU DONE IN THE ARMY?
TWENTY YEARS, SAME AS EVERYONE ELSE. AND TOMORROW JULIUS CAESAR'S GIVING US OUR HONESTA MISSIO!* WITH A FREE GIFT OF A PLOT OF LAND TOO!
* DEMOB
JULIUSH CAESAR! HUH! WANT TO KNOW WHAT I THINK OF JULIUSH CAESAR?

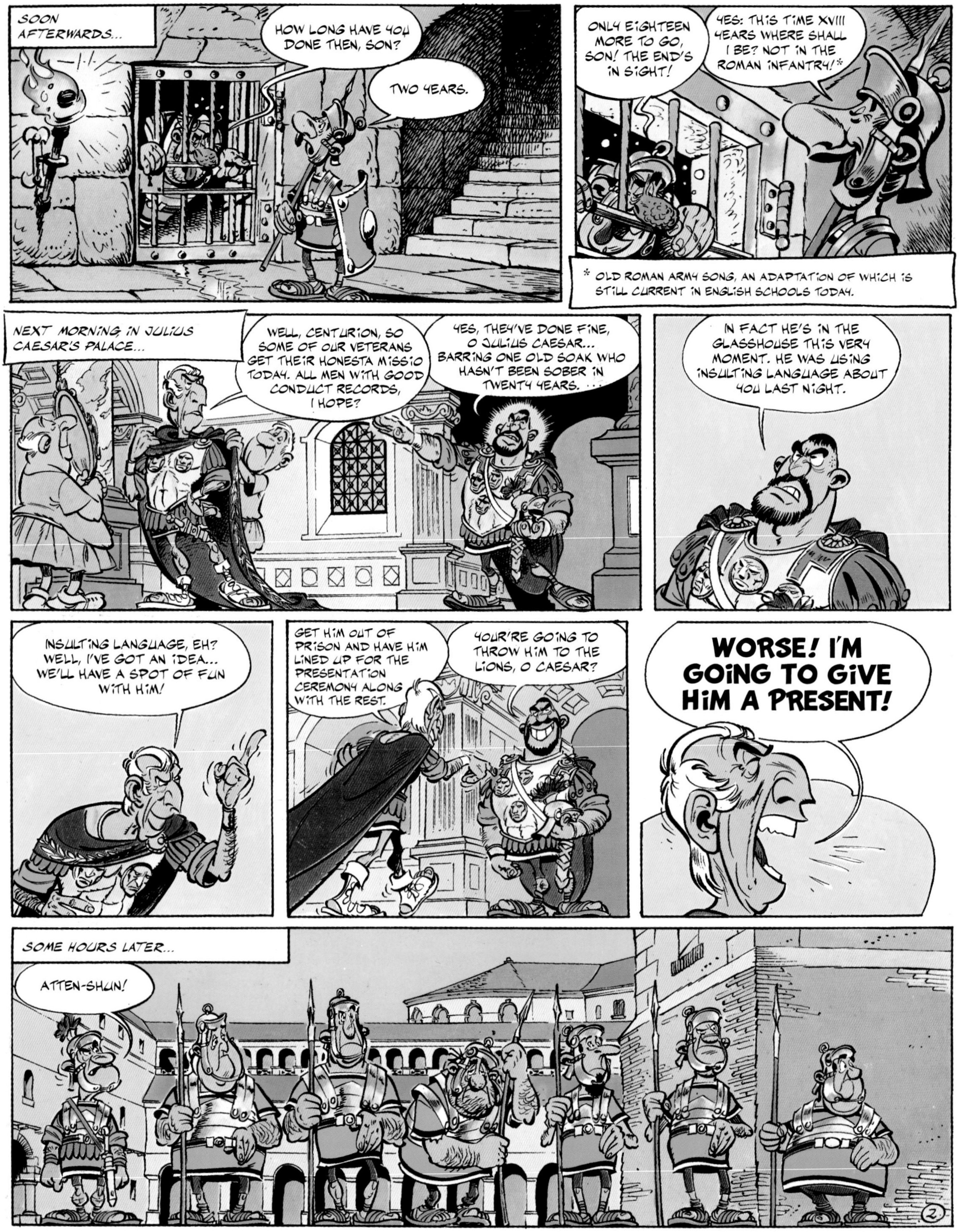
SOON AFTERWARDS...
HOW LONG HAVE YOU DONE THEN, SON?
TWO YEARS.
ONLY EIGHTEEN MORE TO GO, SON! THE END'S IN SIGHT!
YES: THIS TIME XVIII YEARS WHERE SHALL I BE? NOT IN THE ROMAN INFANTRY!*
* OLD ROMAN ARMY SONG, AN ADAPTATION OF WHICH IS STILL CURRENT IN ENGLISH SCHOOLS TODAY.
NEXT MORNING IN JULIUS CAESAR'S PALACE...
WELL, CENTURION, SO SOME OF OUR VETERANS GET THEIR HONESTA MISSIO TODAY. ALL MEN WITH GOOD CONDUCT RECORDS, I HOPE?
YES, THEY'VE DONE FINE, O JULIUS CAESAR... BARRING ONE OLD SOAK WHO HASN'T BEEN SOBER IN TWENTY YEARS.
IN FACT HE'S IN THE GLASSHOUSE THIS VERY MOMENT. HE WAS USING INSULTING LANGUAGE ABOUT YOU LAST NIGHT.
INSULTING LANGUAGE, EH? WELL, I'VE GOT AN IDEA... WE'LL HAVE A SPOT OF FUN WITH HIM!
GET HIM OUT OF PRISON AND HAVE HIM LINED UP FOR THE PRESENTATION CEREMONY ALONG WITH THE REST.
YOUR'RE GOING TO THROW HIM TO THE LIONS, O CAESAR?
WORSE! I'M GOING TO GIVE HIM A PRESENT!
SOME HOURS LATER...
ATTEN-SHUN!
2

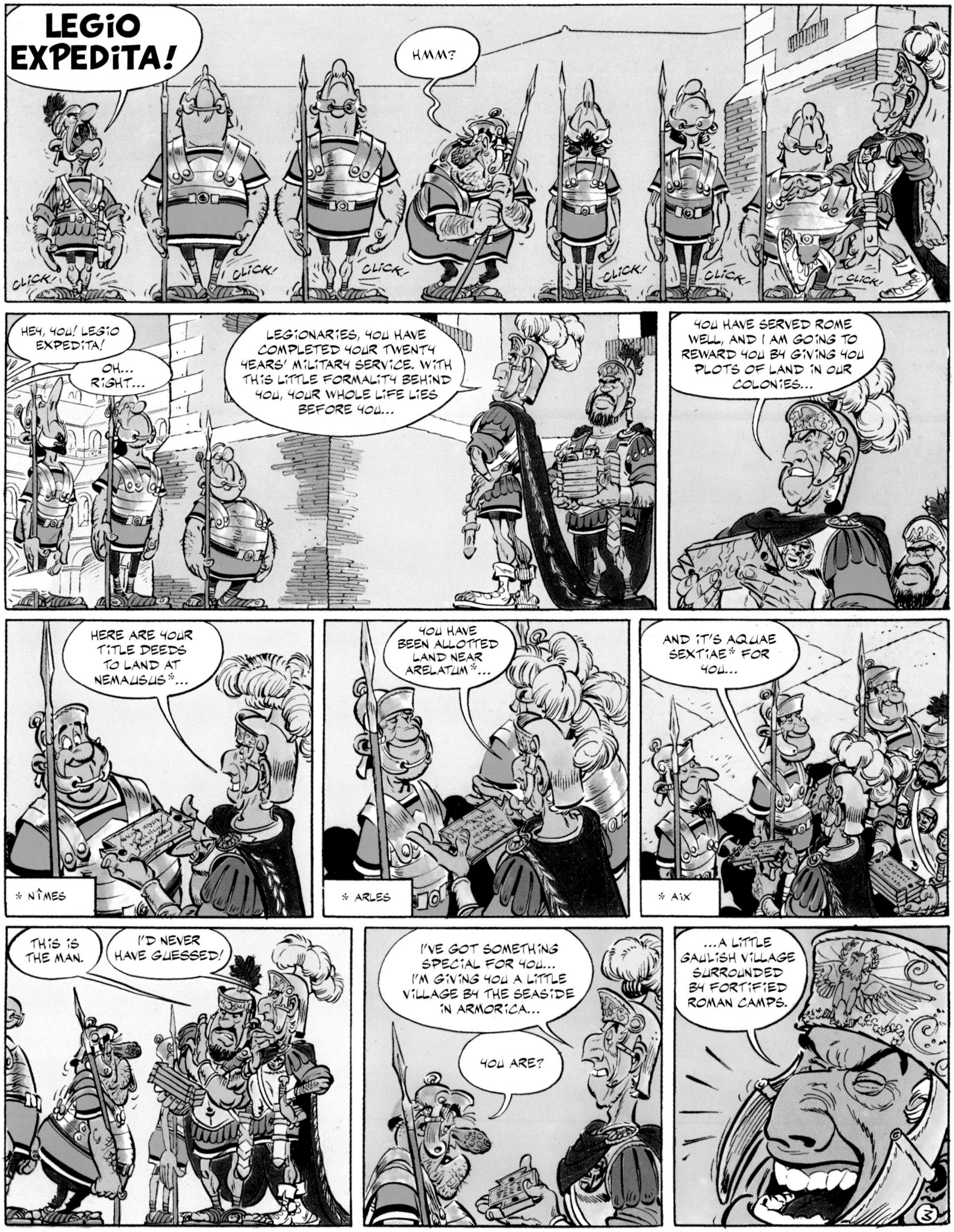
LEGIO EXPEDITA!
HMM?
CLICK!
CLICK!
CLICK!
CLICK!
CLICK!
CLICK!
HEY, YOU! LEGIO EXPEDITA!
OH... RIGHT...
LEGIONARIES, YOU HAVE COMPLETED YOUR TWENTY YEARS' MILITARY SERVICE. WITH THIS LITTLE FORMALITY BEHIND YOU, YOUR WHOLE LIFE LIES BEFORE YOU...
YOU HAVE SERVED ROME WELL, AND I AM GOING TO REWARD YOU BY GIVING YOU PLOTS OF LAND IN OUR COLONIES...
HERE ARE YOUR TITLE DEEDS TO LAND AT NEMAUSUS*...
* NÎMES
YOU HAVE BEEN ALLOTTED LAND NEAR ARELATUM*...
* ARLES
AND IT'S AQUAE SEXTIAE* FOR YOU...
* AIX
THIS IS THE MAN.
I'D NEVER HAVE GUESSED!
I'VE GOT SOMETHING SPECIAL FOR YOU... I'M GIVING YOU A LITTLE VILLAGE BY THE SEASIDE IN ARMORICA...
YOU ARE?
...A LITTLE GAULISH VILLAGE SURROUNDED BY FORTIFIED ROMAN CAMPS.
3

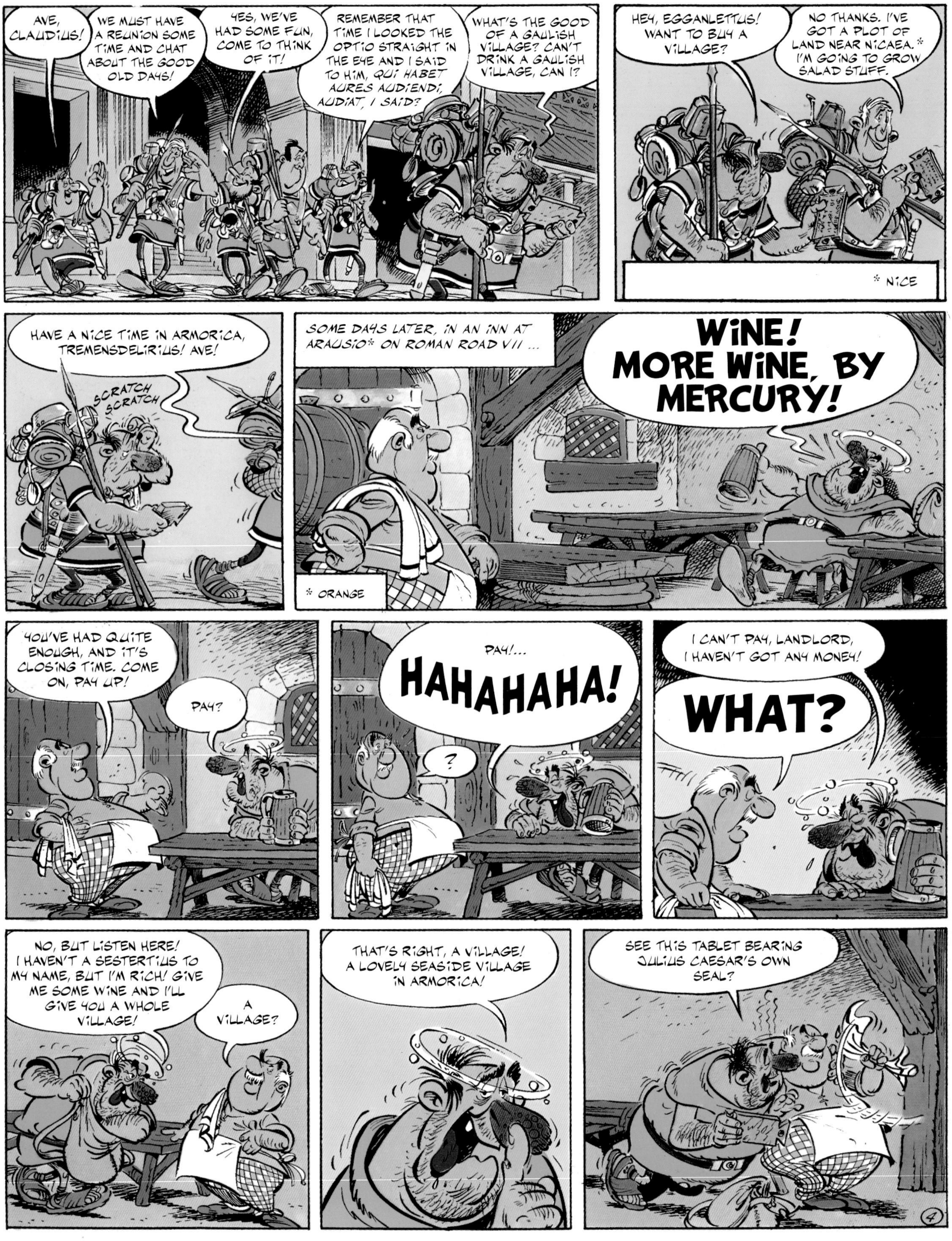
AVE, CLAUDIUS!
WE MUST HAVE A REUNION SOME TIME AND CHAT ABOUT THE GOOD OLD DAYS!
YES, WE'VE HAD SOME FUN, COME TO THINK OF IT!
REMEMBER THAT TIME I LOOKED THE OPTIO STRAIGHT IN THE EYE AND I SAID TO HIM, QUI HABET AURES AUDIENDI, AUDIAT, I SAID?
WHAT'S THE GOOD OF A GAULISH VILLAGE? CAN'T DRINK A GAULISH VILLAGE, CAN I?
HEY, EGGANLETTUS! WANT TO BUY A VILLAGE?
NO THANKS. I'VE GOT A PLOT OF LAND NEAR NICAEA.* I'M GOING TO GROW SALAD STUFF.
* NICE
HAVE A NICE TIME IN ARMORICA, TREMENSDELIRIUS! AVE!
SCRATCH SCRATCH
SOME DAYS LATER, IN AN INN AT ARAUSIO* ON ROMAN ROAD VII ...
WINE! MORE WINE, BY MERCURY!
* ORANGE
YOU'VE HAD QUITE ENOUGH, AND IT'S CLOSING TIME. COME ON, PAY UP!
PAY?
PAY!... HAHAHAHA!
?
I CAN'T PAY, LANDLORD, I HAVEN'T GOT ANY MONEY!
WHAT?
NO, BUT LISTEN HERE! I HAVEN'T A SESTERTIUS TO MY NAME, BUT I'M RICH! GIVE ME SOME WINE AND I'LL GIVE YOU A WHOLE VILLAGE!
A VILLAGE?
THAT'S RIGHT, A VILLAGE! A LOVELY SEASIDE VILLAGE IN ARMORICA!
SEE THIS TABLET BEARING JULIUS CAESAR'S OWN SEAL?
4

YOU MEAN YOU'D GIVE ME THIS VILLAGE, JUST FOR THE PRICE OF A MEAL AND A LITTLE WINE?

I MUST ASK MY WIFE.

DON'T FORGET THE WINE ON YOUR WAY BACK.

...AND LOOK AT THIS! AN OFFICIAL DOCUMENT! WITH JULIUS CAESAR'S OWN SEAL! I'VE ALWAYS DREAMT OF OWNING LAND...

I MUST ADMIT, IT'S TEMPTING... THE CLIMATE HERE DOESN'T REALLY SUIT ME, SEASIDE AIR IS SO BRACING, AND WHAT'S MORE, AN INN IS NO FIT PLACE TO BRING UP A YOUNG GIRL...

WELL, ANGINA?

SPECIALLY AS OUR LITTLE INFLUENZA WAS NEVER HAPPY ABOUT LEAVING LUTETIA TO COME HERE.

WE COULD SELL THIS INN...

WELL?

IT'S A DEAL!

FILL IT UP!

AS IT HAPPENS... THE LITTLE VILLAGE WHICH HAS CHANGED HANDS FOR A HUNK OF BREAD AND A FEW MUGS OF WINE...

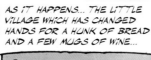
...IS THIS VILLAGE!

GAULISH VILLAGE
COMPENDIUM
LAUDANUM
AQUARIUM
TOTORUM

⑤

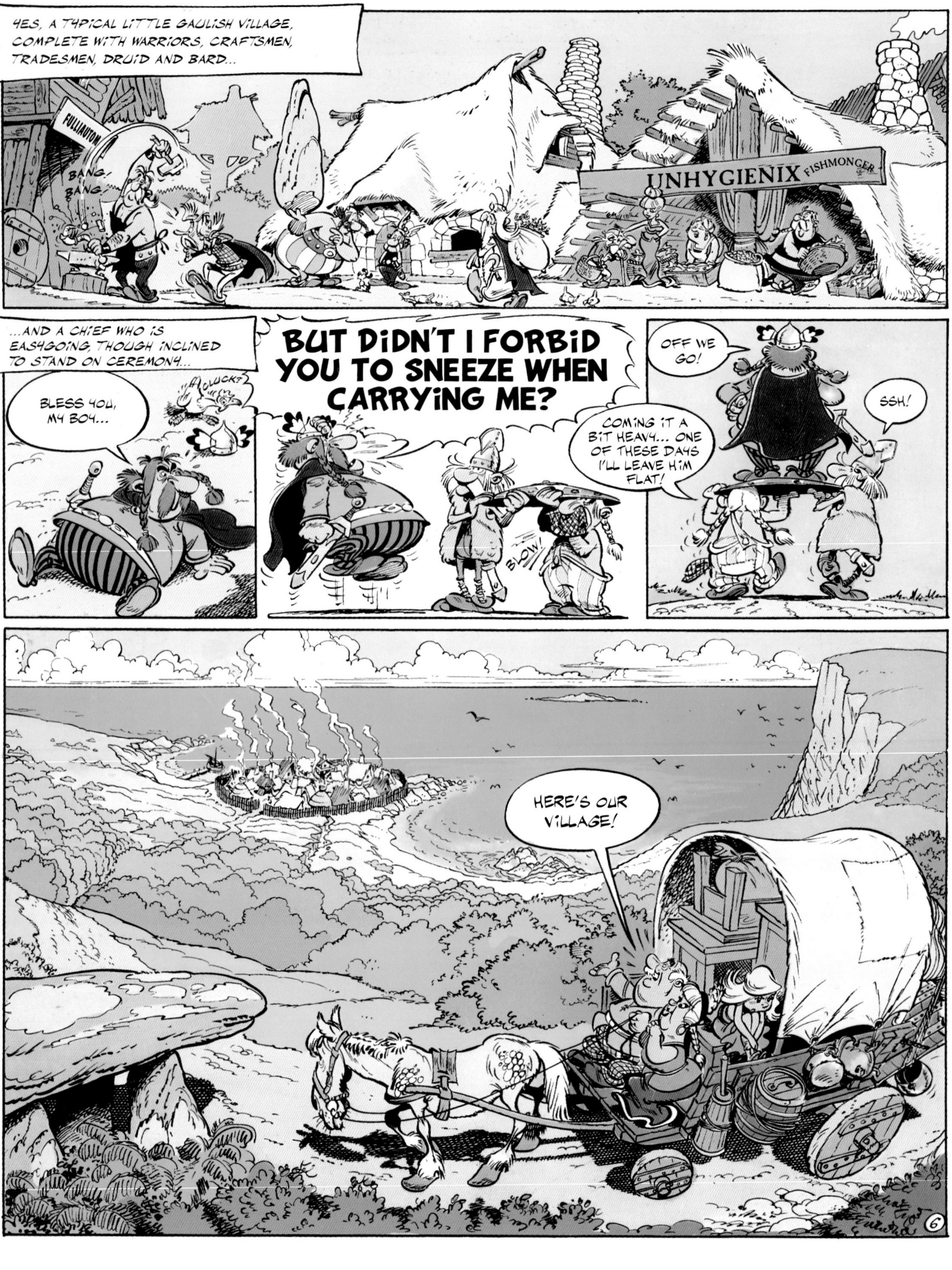

YES, A TYPICAL LITTLE GAULISH VILLAGE, COMPLETE WITH WARRIORS, CRAFTSMEN, TRADESMEN, DRUID AND BARD...
BANG- BANG-
UNHYGIENIX FISHMONGER
...AND A CHIEF WHO IS EASYGOING, THOUGH INCLINED TO STAND ON CEREMONY...
BLESS YOU, MY BOY...
CLUCK?
BUT DIDN'T I FORBID YOU TO SNEEZE WHEN CARRYING ME?
BLOW!
COMING IT A BIT HEAVY... ONE OF THESE DAYS I'LL LEAVE HIM FLAT!
OFF WE GO!
SSH!
HERE'S OUR VILLAGE!

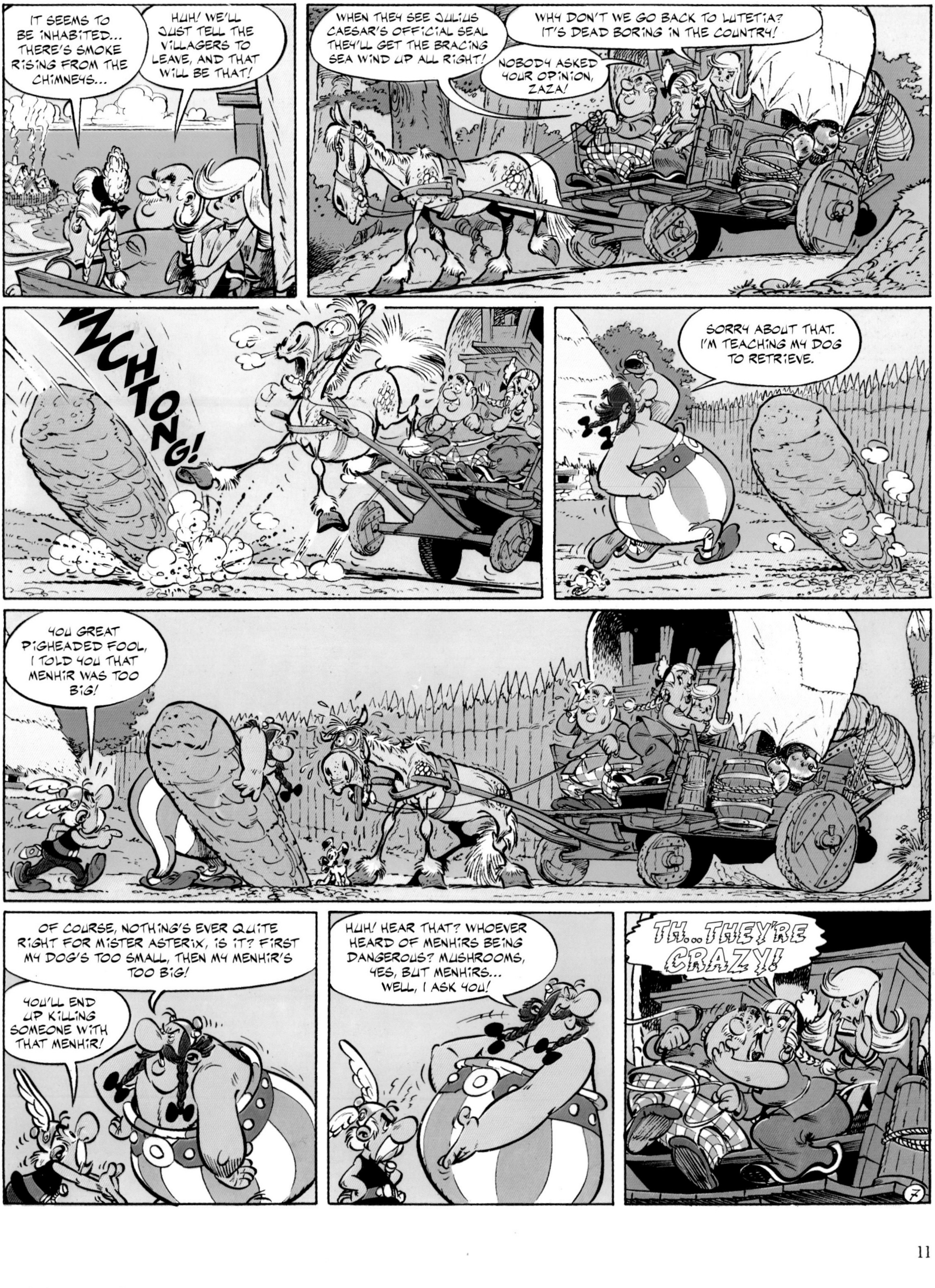

IT SEEMS TO BE INHABITED... THERE'S SMOKE RISING FROM THE CHIMNEYS...
HUH! WE'LL JUST TELL THE VILLAGERS TO LEAVE, AND THAT WILL BE THAT!
WHEN THEY SEE JULIUS CAESAR'S OFFICIAL SEAL THEY'LL GET THE BRACING SEA WIND UP ALL RIGHT!
WHY DON'T WE GO BACK TO LUTETIA? IT'S DEAD BORING IN THE COUNTRY!
NOBODY ASKED YOUR OPINION, ZAZA!
NCHTONG!
SORRY ABOUT THAT. I'M TEACHING MY DOG TO RETRIEVE.
YOU GREAT PIGHEADED FOOL, I TOLD YOU THAT MENHIR WAS TOO BIG!
OF COURSE, NOTHING'S EVER QUITE RIGHT FOR MISTER ASTERIX, IS IT? FIRST MY DOG'S TOO SMALL, THEN MY MENHIR'S TOO BIG!
YOU'LL END UP KILLING SOMEONE WITH THAT MENHIR!
HUH! HEAR THAT? WHOEVER HEARD OF MENHIRS BEING DANGEROUS? MUSHROOMS, YES, BUT MENHIRS... WELL, I ASK YOU!
TH... THEY'RE CRAZY!
7

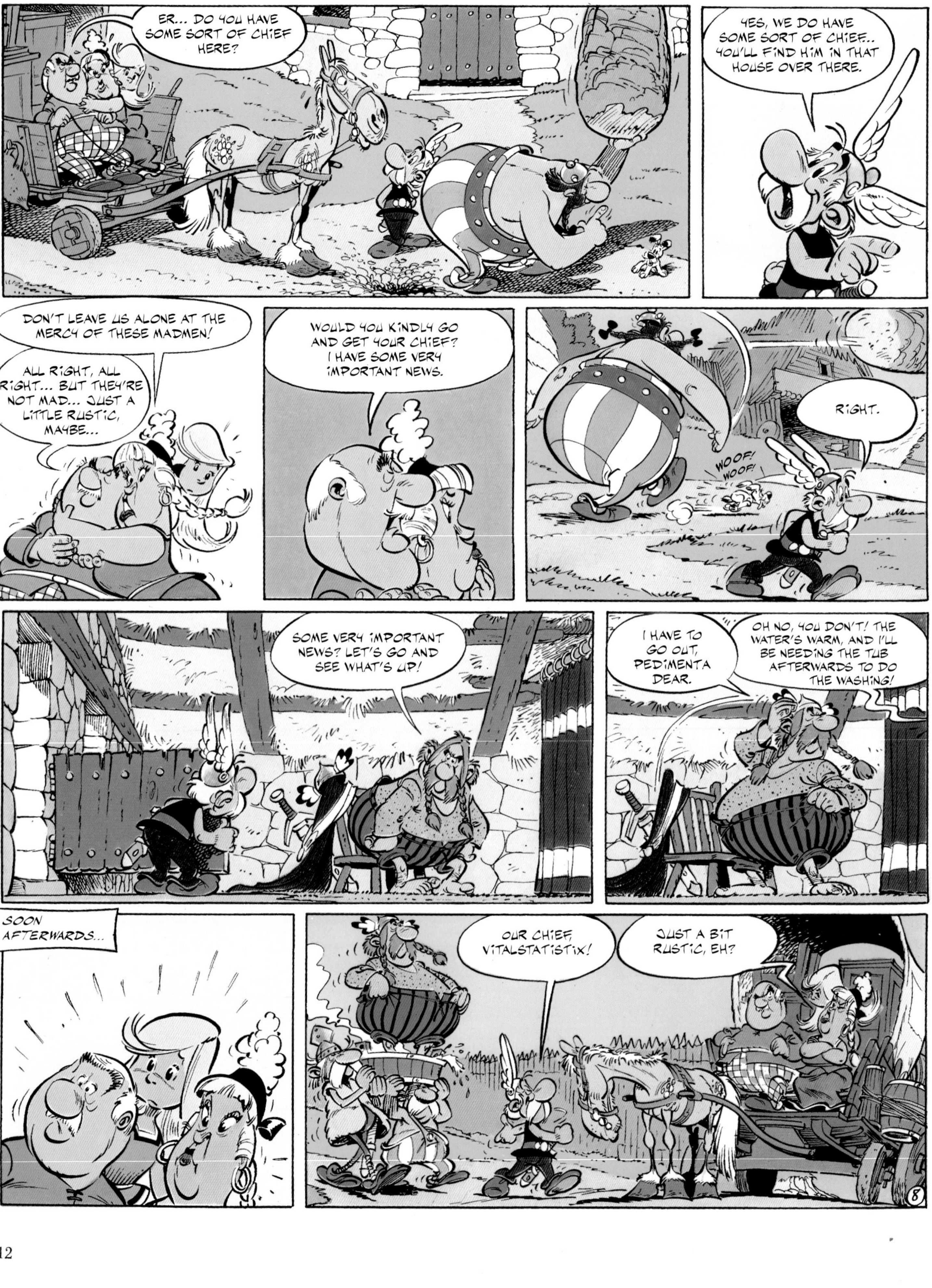

ER... DO YOU HAVE SOME SORT OF CHIEF HERE?
YES, WE DO HAVE SOME SORT OF CHIEF.. YOU'LL FIND HIM IN THAT HOUSE OVER THERE.
DON'T LEAVE US ALONE AT THE MERCY OF THESE MADMEN!
ALL RIGHT, ALL RIGHT... BUT THEY'RE NOT MAD... JUST A LITTLE RUSTIC, MAYBE...
WOULD YOU KINDLY GO AND GET YOUR CHIEF? I HAVE SOME VERY IMPORTANT NEWS.
RIGHT.
WOOF! WOOF!
SOME VERY IMPORTANT NEWS? LET'S GO AND SEE WHAT'S UP!
I HAVE TO GO OUT, PEDIMENTA DEAR.
OH NO, YOU DON'T! THE WATER'S WARM, AND I'LL BE NEEDING THE TUB AFTERWARDS TO DO THE WASHING!
SOON AFTERWARDS...
OUR CHIEF, VITALSTATISTIX!
JUST A BIT RUSTIC, EH?
8

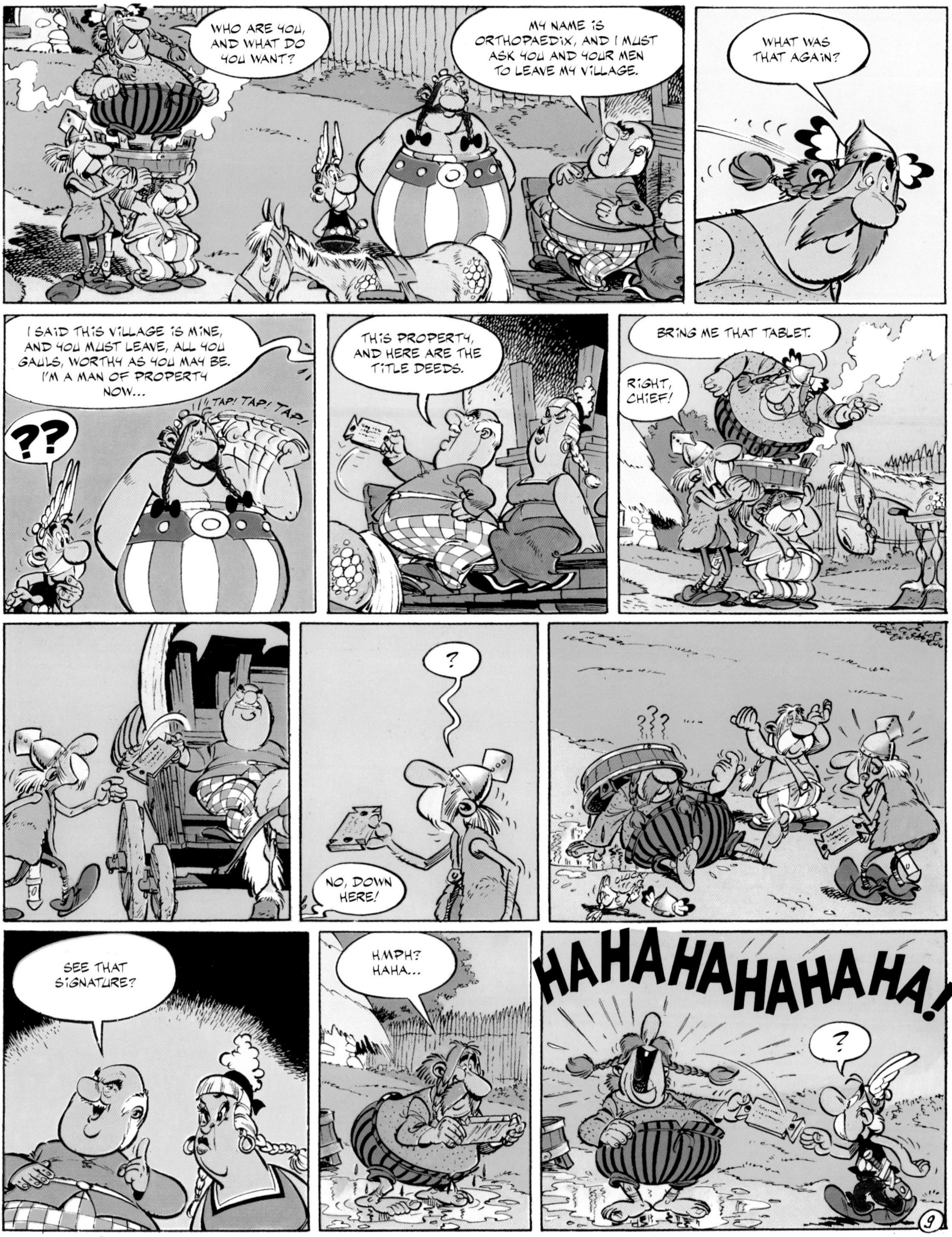
WHO ARE YOU, AND WHAT DO YOU WANT?
MY NAME IS ORTHOPAEDIX, AND I MUST ASK YOU AND YOUR MEN TO LEAVE MY VILLAGE.
WHAT WAS THAT AGAIN?
I SAID THIS VILLAGE IS MINE, AND YOU MUST LEAVE, ALL YOU GAULS, WORTHY AS YOU MAY BE. I'M A MAN OF PROPERTY NOW...
??
TAP! TAP! TAP!
THIS PROPERTY, AND HERE ARE THE TITLE DEEDS.
BRING ME THAT TABLET.
RIGHT, CHIEF!
?
NO, DOWN HERE!
???
CLUCK
SEE THAT SIGNATURE?
HMPH? HAHA...
HAHAHAHAHAHAHA!
?

AHAHAHAHAHAH!

CLUCK?

JOKING APART, MATE, YOU'VE BEEN HAD!

WHAT ABOUT THIS TABLET? SEE THAT SIGNATURE?

YOU CAN'T GIVE AWAY WHAT ISN'T YOURS, AND JULIUS CAESAR OWNS ALL GAUL... EXCEPT THIS VILLAGE!

GOODBYE, AND GOOD LUCK!

LONG LIVE CHIEF VITALSTATISTIX!

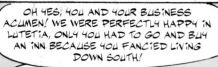

OH YES, YOU AND YOUR BUSINESS ACUMEN! WE WERE PERFECTLY HAPPY IN LUTETIA, ONLY YOU HAD TO GO AND BUY AN INN BECAUSE YOU FANCIED LIVING DOWN SOUTH!

PLEASE... GINA DEAR...

A FAT LOT YOU CARED THAT THE CLIMATE DIDN'T SUIT ME AND IT WAS NO FIT PLACE TO BRING UP INFLUENZA!

AND THEN YOU GO CHUCKING IT ALL UP AGAIN, JUST FOR A WORTHLESS SCRAP OF MARBLE! WHEN I THINK OF MY SISTER WHO MARRIED DITHYRAMBIX...

DITHYRAMBIX IS A FOOL!

HE MAY BE A FOOL, BUT HE'S A RICH FOOL! HE'S MADE GOOD! OH, MY POOR DEAR MOTHER WAS RIGHT ALL ALONG...!

COME HERE A MINUTE, ORTHOPAEDIX.

?

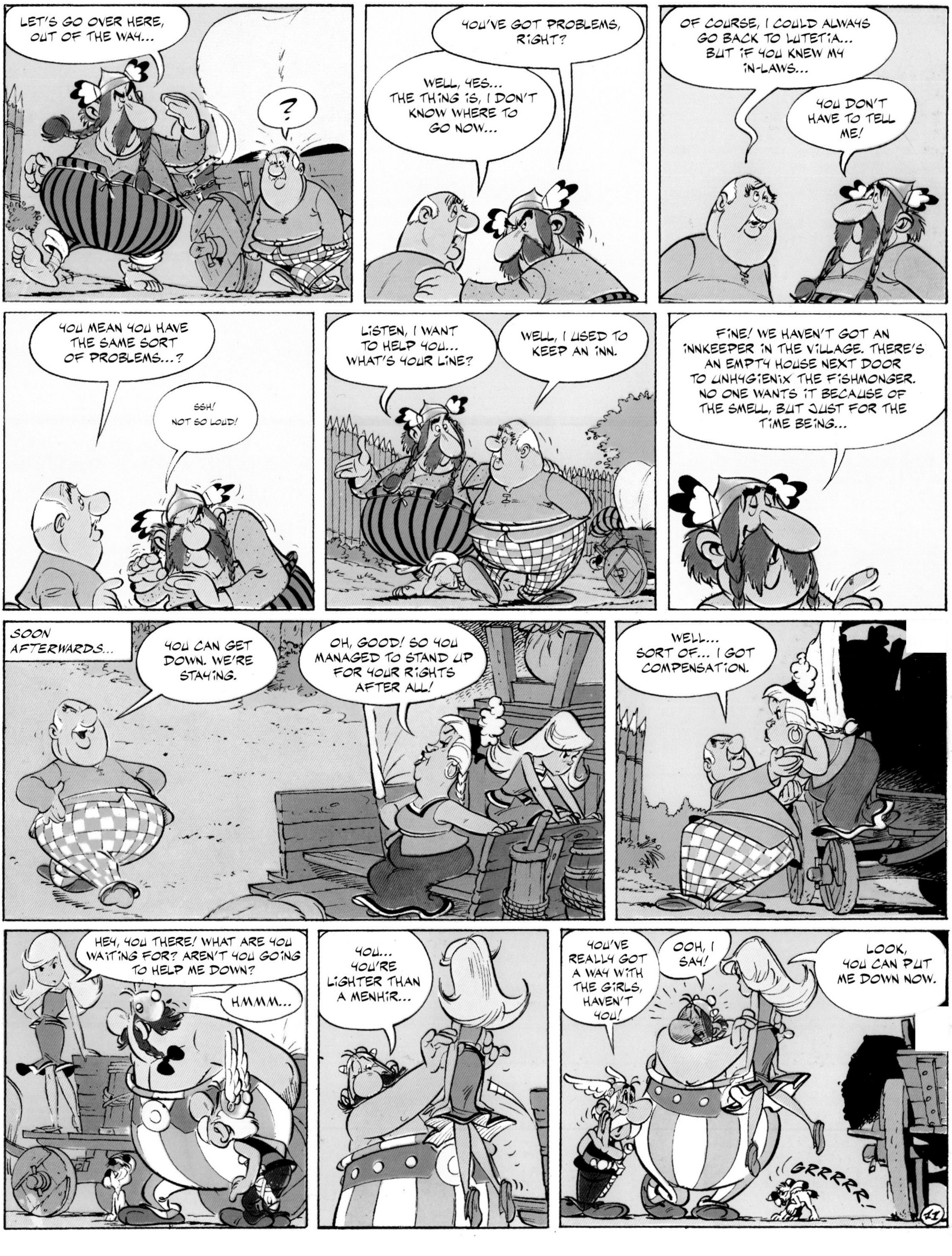
LET'S GO OVER HERE, OUT OF THE WAY...
?
YOU'VE GOT PROBLEMS, RIGHT?
WELL, YES... THE THING IS, I DON'T KNOW WHERE TO GO NOW...
OF COURSE, I COULD ALWAYS GO BACK TO LUTETIA... BUT IF YOU KNEW MY IN-LAWS...
YOU DON'T HAVE TO TELL ME!
YOU MEAN YOU HAVE THE SAME SORT OF PROBLEMS...?
SSH! NOT SO LOUD!
LISTEN, I WANT TO HELP YOU... WHAT'S YOUR LINE?
WELL, I USED TO KEEP AN INN.
FINE! WE HAVEN'T GOT AN INNKEEPER IN THE VILLAGE. THERE'S AN EMPTY HOUSE NEXT DOOR TO UNHYGIENIX THE FISHMONGER. NO ONE WANTS IT BECAUSE OF THE SMELL, BUT JUST FOR THE TIME BEING...
SOON AFTERWARDS...
YOU CAN GET DOWN. WE'RE STAYING.
OH, GOOD! SO YOU MANAGED TO STAND UP FOR YOUR RIGHTS AFTER ALL!
WELL... SORT OF... I GOT COMPENSATION.
HEY, YOU THERE! WHAT ARE YOU WAITING FOR? AREN'T YOU GOING TO HELP ME DOWN?
HMMM...
YOU... YOU'RE LIGHTER THAN A MENHIR...
YOU'VE REALLY GOT A WAY WITH THE GIRLS, HAVEN'T YOU!
OOH, I SAY!
LOOK, YOU CAN PUT ME DOWN NOW.
GRRRRR-
11

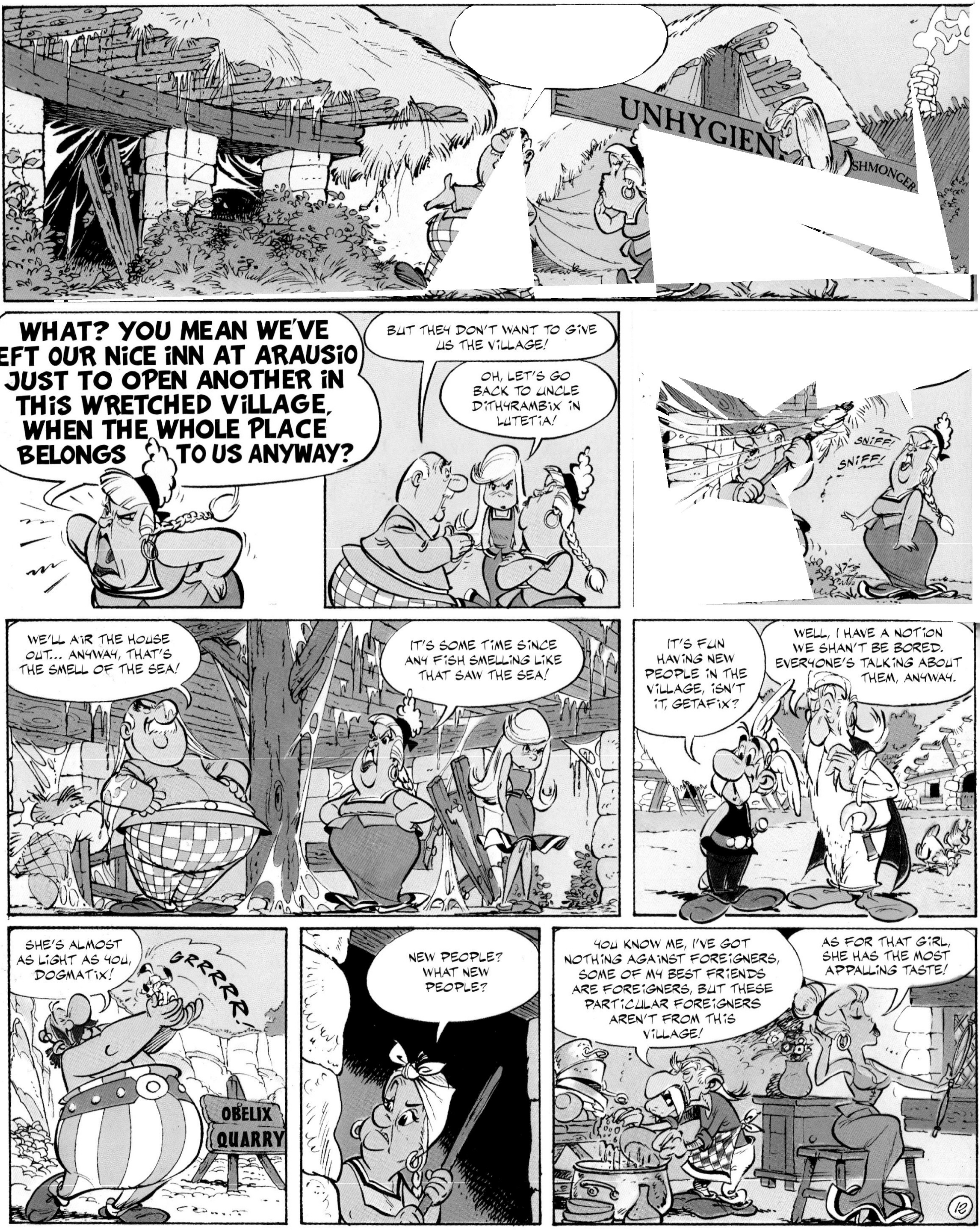
UNHYGIEN
SHMONGER
WHAT? YOU MEAN WE'VE LEFT OUR NICE INN AT ARAUSIO JUST TO OPEN ANOTHER IN THIS WRETCHED VILLAGE, WHEN THE WHOLE PLACE BELONGS TO US ANYWAY?
BUT THEY DON'T WANT TO GIVE US THE VILLAGE!
OH, LET'S GO BACK TO UNCLE DITHYRAMBIX IN LUTETIA!
SNIFF!
SNIFF!
WE'LL AIR THE HOUSE OUT... ANYWAY, THAT'S THE SMELL OF THE SEA!
IT'S SOME TIME SINCE ANY FISH SMELLING LIKE THAT SAW THE SEA!
IT'S FUN HAVING NEW PEOPLE IN THE VILLAGE, ISN'T IT, GETAFIX?
WELL, I HAVE A NOTION WE SHAN'T BE BORED. EVERYONE'S TALKING ABOUT THEM, ANYWAY.
SHE'S ALMOST AS LIGHT AS YOU, DOGMATIX!
GRRRRR!
OBELIX QUARRY
NEW PEOPLE? WHAT NEW PEOPLE?
YOU KNOW ME, I'VE GOT NOTHING AGAINST FOREIGNERS, SOME OF MY BEST FRIENDS ARE FOREIGNERS, BUT THESE PARTICULAR FOREIGNERS AREN'T FROM THIS VILLAGE!
AS FOR THAT GIRL, SHE HAS THE MOST APPALLING TASTE!

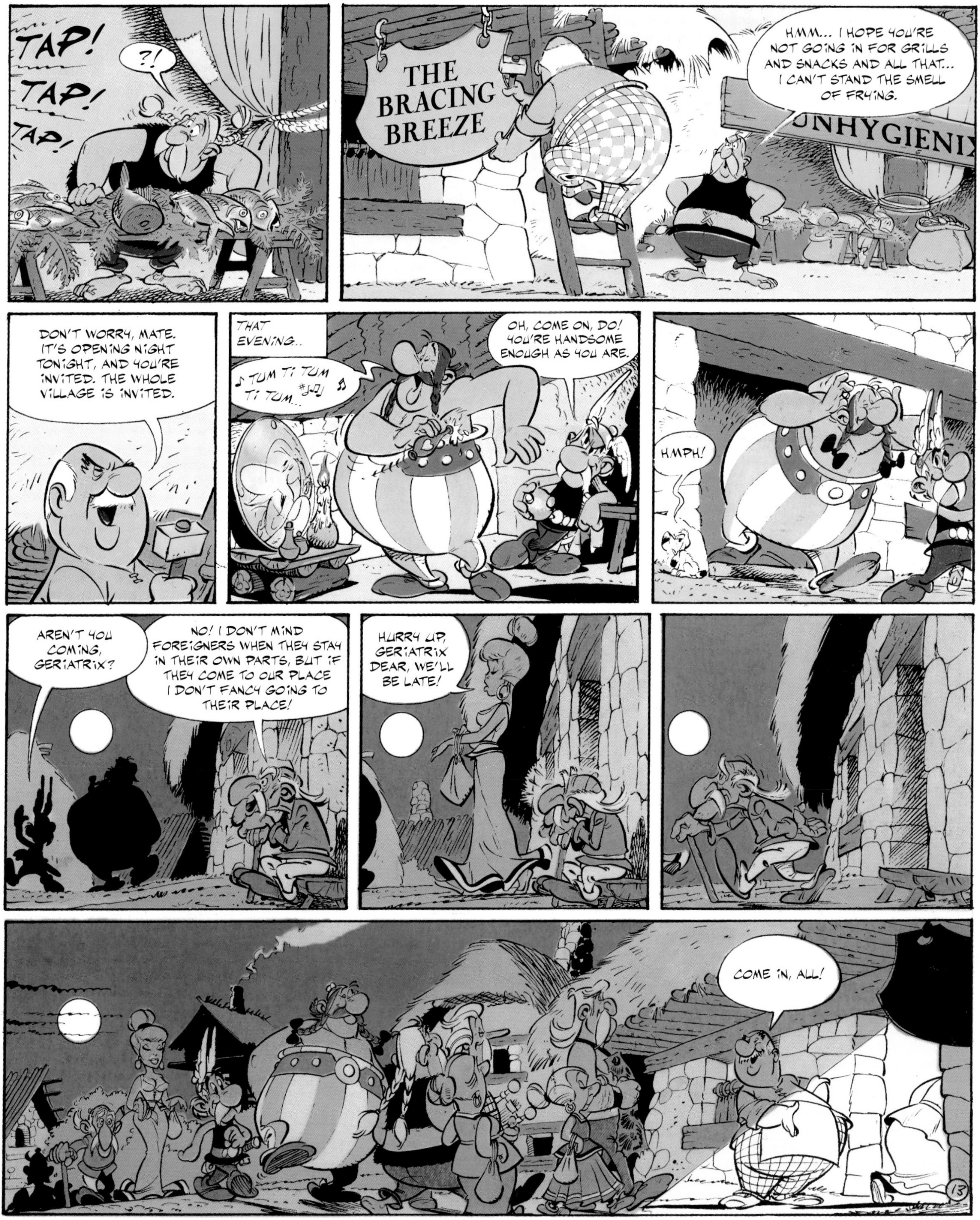
TAP!
TAP!
TAP!
?!
THE BRACING BREEZE
HMM... I HOPE YOU'RE NOT GOING IN FOR GRILLS AND SNACKS AND ALL THAT... I CAN'T STAND THE SMELL OF FRYING.
UNHYGIENIX
DON'T WORRY, MATE. IT'S OPENING NIGHT TONIGHT, AND YOU'RE INVITED. THE WHOLE VILLAGE IS INVITED.
THAT EVENING...
TUM TI TUM TI TUM...
OH, COME ON, DO! YOU'RE HANDSOME ENOUGH AS YOU ARE.
HMPH!
AREN'T YOU COMING, GERIATRIX?
NO! I DON'T MIND FOREIGNERS WHEN THEY STAY IN THEIR OWN PARTS, BUT IF THEY COME TO OUR PLACE I DON'T FANCY GOING TO THEIR PLACE!
HURRY UP, GERIATRIX DEAR, WE'LL BE LATE!
COME IN, ALL!
13

IMPEDIMENTA, MEET OUR NEW INNKEEPER, ORTHOPAEDIX.

PLEASED TO MEET YOU.

PLEASED TO MEET YOU.

NICE LITTLE PLACE YOU HAVE HERE, MRS ORTHOPAEDIX. WHAT A PITY ABOUT THE SMELL OF FISH.

FISH!

WE WERE OBLIGED TO TAKE WHAT WAS OFFERED, MRS VITALSTATISTIX. I DARE SAY YOUR PLAICE SMELLS BETTER.

NATURALLY, MRS ORTHOPAEDIX. AFTER ALL, I'M THE CHIEF'S WIFE!

IT DOESN'T HALF SMELL OF FISH, TOO!

OH, SO IT SMELLS OF FISH, EH?

WHAT CHIEF'S WIFE, MRS VITALSTATISTIX? THIS VILLAGE BELONGS TO MY HUSBAND.

ANGINA, DEAR, COME AND HELP ME SERVE OUR GUESTS.

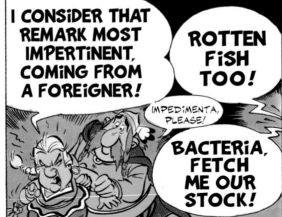

I CONSIDER THAT REMARK MOST IMPERTINENT, COMING FROM A FOREIGNER!

ROTTEN FISH TOO!

IMPEDIMENTA, PLEASE!

BACTERIA, FETCH ME OUR STOCK!

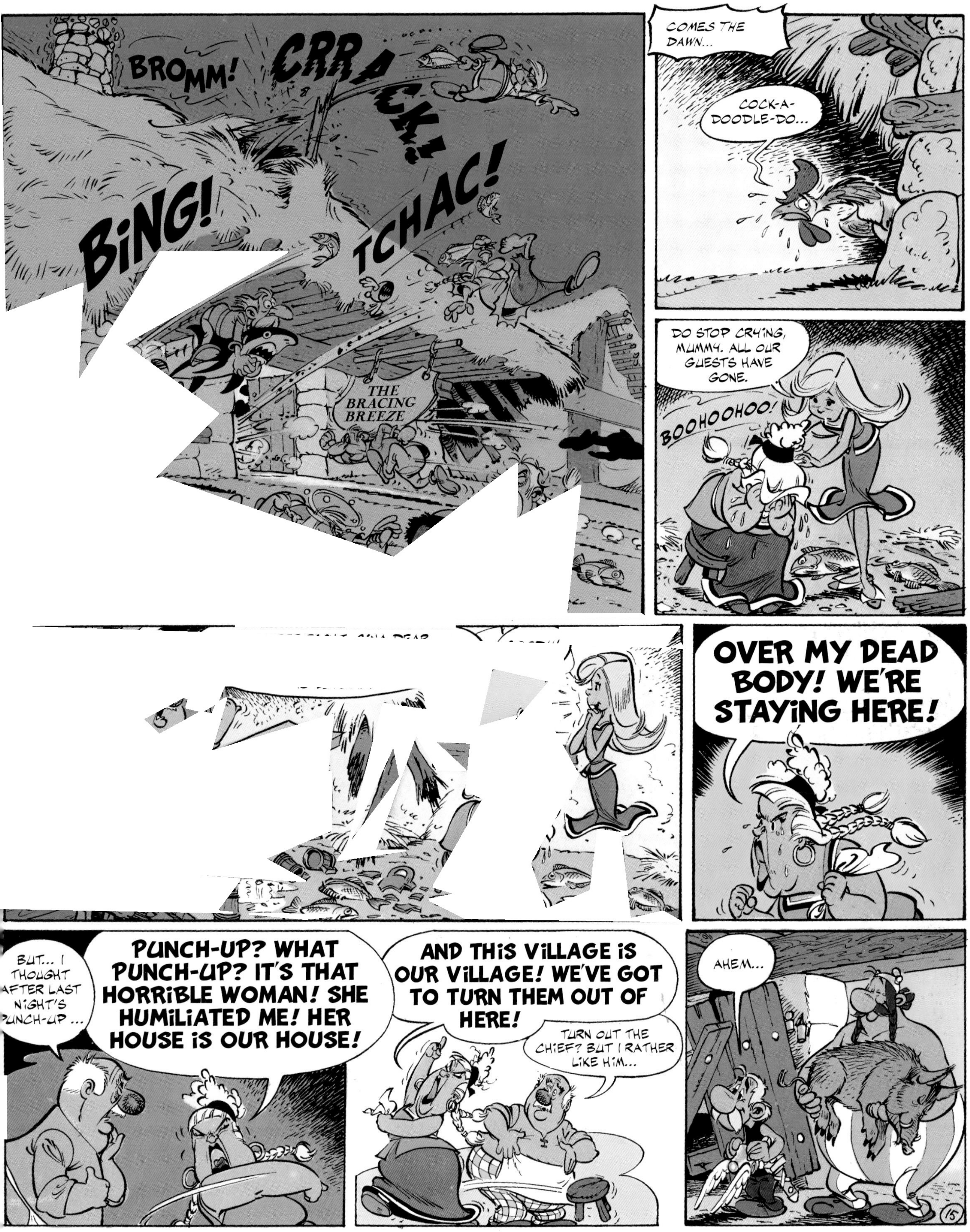

BROMM!
CRRACK!
BING!
TCHAC!
THE BRACING BREEZE
COMES THE DAWN...
COCK-A-DOODLE-DO...
DO STOP CRYING, MUMMY. ALL OUR GUESTS HAVE GONE.
BOOHOOHOO!
OVER MY DEAD BODY! WE'RE STAYING HERE!
BUT... I THOUGHT AFTER LAST NIGHT'S PUNCH-UP ...
PUNCH-UP? WHAT PUNCH-UP? IT'S THAT HORRIBLE WOMAN! SHE HUMILIATED ME! HER HOUSE IS OUR HOUSE!
AND THIS VILLAGE IS OUR VILLAGE! WE'VE GOT TO TURN THEM OUT OF HERE!
TURN OUT THE CHIEF? BUT I RATHER LIKE HIM...
AHEM...
15

WE'VE COME TO HELP YOU CLEAR UP THE MESS... OUR FRIENDS MEAN WELL, YOU KNOW. THEY'RE JUST A BIT HIGH-SPIRITED, THAT'S ALL...

AND I'VE BROUGHT YOU A BOAR FOR BREAKFAST.

I DON'T THINK THIS IS QUITE THE MOMENT ...

OH YES IT IS! WE SHAN'T FORGET YOUR KIND GESTURE...

ESPECIALLY AS MY SBAND ORTHOPAEDIX ITENDS TO BECOME CHIEF OF THIS VILLAGE.

WHAT? CHIEF OF THIS VILLAGE? HOW ABOUT ME?

OUR LAWS CLEARLY STATE THAT ANYONE AT ALL HAS THE RIGHT TO STAND FOR ELECTION. IF HE GETS A MAJORITY VOTE, HE TAKES OVER FROM THE OLD CHIEF.

I'M GOING TO FLING HIM OUT OF THE VILLAGE, I AM!

OH, LET HIM MAKE A FOOL OF HIMSELF. WHEN HE FINDS NO ONE WANTS HIM FOR CHIEF HE'LL LEAVE, ALONG WITH THAT FAT WIFE OF HIS!

ORTHOPAEDIX!

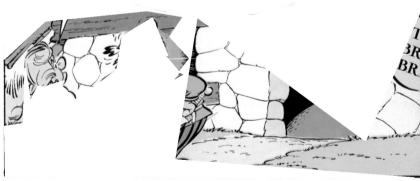

SO YOU'RE THINKING OF TAKING OVER FROM ME AS CHIEF?

ER...

THAT'S RIGHT!

WHAT DO YOU MEAN, WHY DON'T I SHUT UP? THIS IS MAN'S WORK!

ORTHO-PAEDIX! ARE YOU GOING TO LET HER SPEAK TO ME LIKE THAT?

ER... WELL... NO.

THE FESTIVAL OF THE GOD LUG IS IN FIFTEEN DAYS' TIME! IF YOUR FOOL OF A HUSBAND GETS MORE VOTES THAN MINE THEN, AND ONLY THEN, HE BECOMES CHIEF OF OUR VILLAGE!

WHAT?

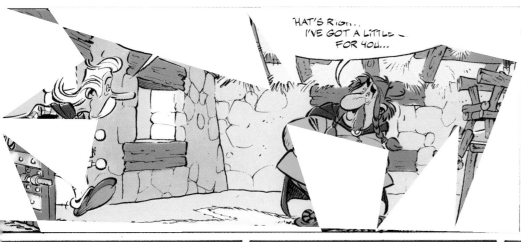

HAT'S RIGHT... I'VE GOT A LITTLE — FOR YOU...

IT'S NOT THAT I DOUBT THEIR LOYALTY, EXACTLY, BUT I'D LIKE YOU TO SOUND OUT OUR FRIENDS: SEE IF THEY WANT A CHANGE OF CHIEF.

LATER...

WELL, WHAT NEWS?

GERIATRIX IS BACKING YOU. HE SAYS HE'S GOT NOTHING AGAINST FOREIGNERS BUT THEY DON'T BELONG HERE. THE OTHERS DON'T MIND ONE WAY OR THE OTHER, SO LONG AS THEY STILL GET PLENTY OF BOARS AND ROMANS...

FULLIAUTOMATIX THOUGHT I WAS GOING TO SOUND HIM OUT IN SONG, SO HE KNOCKED ME OUT FIRST.

YOU HAVEN'T VOICED YOUR OWN OPINION YET...?

HUH! YOU DON'T LIKE MY VOICE ANY MORE THAN THE REST OF THEM!

WHAT, ME? I SIMPLY LOVE YOUR VOICE!

YOU DO? LISTEN TO THIS NEW PROTEST SONG I'VE JUST COMPOSED, THEN...

SPLOIIING!

CLOIIK!

WE SHALL OVERCOME... WE SHALL OVER-COME...

FREEDOM FIGHTERS THE WORLD OVER OWE THIS SONG TO CACOFONIX. THE ORIGINAL TUNE HAS, OF COURSE, BEEN EXTENSIVELY REVISED...

STOP! I'M OVERCOME ALREADY! THIS IS A PROTEST... MARCH!

ALL RIGHT, ORTHOPAEDIX CAN HAVE THE BENEFIT OF MY SONG! MAYBE HE'LL APPRECIATE IT!!!

PEDIMENTA, I FEEL WE MAY HAVE MADE A MISTAKE... THAT'S ONE PROTEST VOTE ALREADY!

WHY NOT ADDRESS YOUR PEOPLE? ROUSE THEM UP A BIT?

21

COME ON, OBELIX. OUR CHIEF WANTS TO ADDRESS US.

I'VE GOT SOME MENHIRS TO DRESS, I HAVE!

MY FRIENDS! CERTAIN PERSONS HAVE DARED TO SUGGEST A CHANGE OF CHIEF!! I KNOW YOU WILL THINK THIS AS FUNNY AS I DO...

FOREIGNERS OUT! FOREIGNERS OUT!

YES, YES, THAT'LL DO, THANK YOU, GERIATRIX.

IF THE SAME OLD CHIEF STAYS IN OFFICE, WILL HE GUARANTEE THE FRESHNESS OF GOODS SOLD BY CERTAIN TRADESMEN? WE WANT CONSUMER PROTECTION!

TAP! TAP! TAP!

!

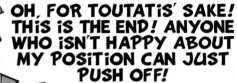

CONSUMER PROTECTION IS UPPERMOST IN MY MIND, FULLIAUTOMATIX!

OH, IT IS, IS IT?

OH, FOR TOUTATIS' SAKE! THIS IS THE END! ANYONE WHO ISN'T HAPPY ABOUT MY POSITION CAN JUST PUSH OFF!

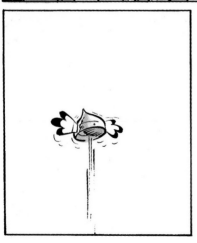

?!

18

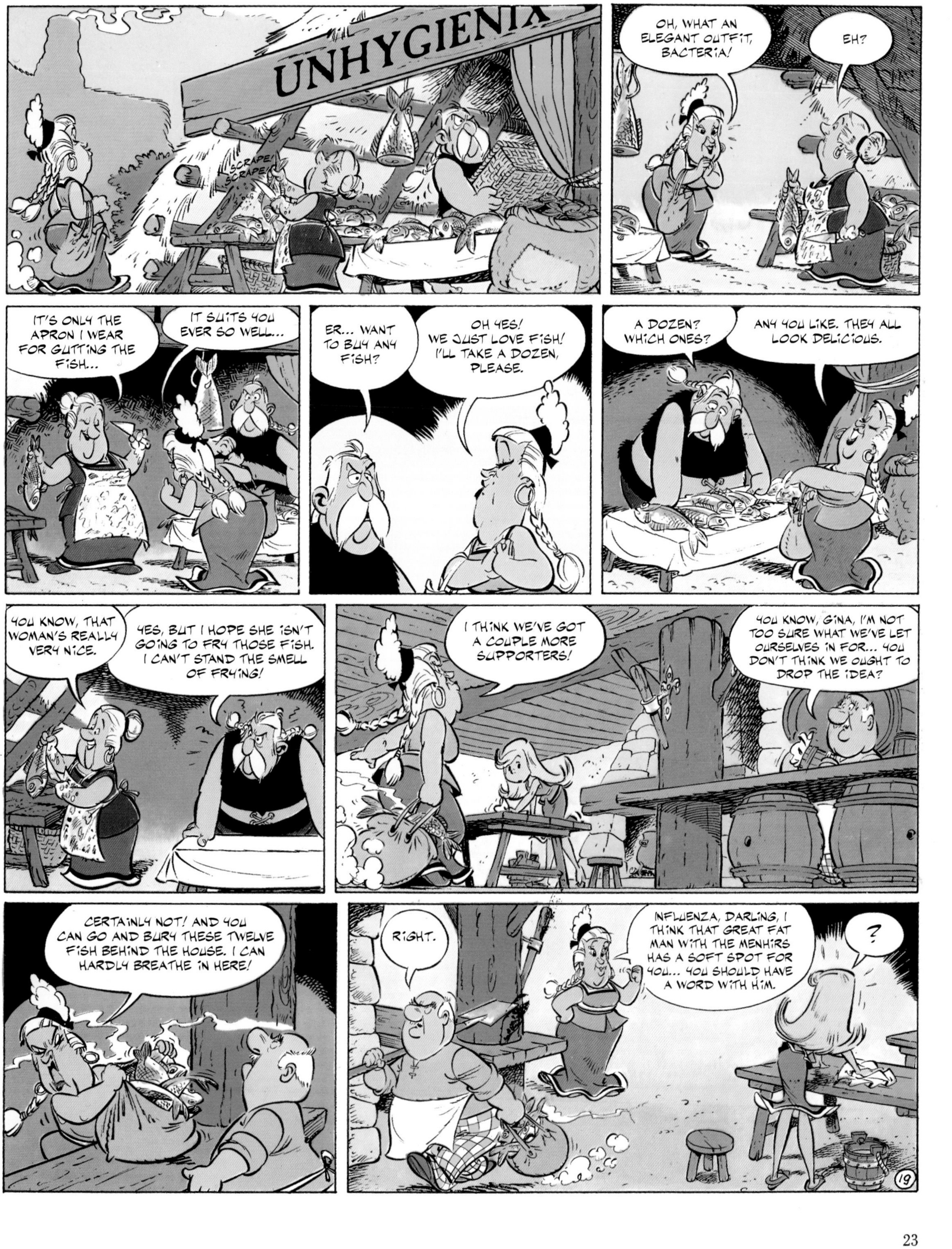
UNHYGIENIX
SCRAPE! SCRAPE!
OH, WHAT AN ELEGANT OUTFIT, BACTERIA!
EH?
IT'S ONLY THE APRON I WEAR FOR GUTTING THE FISH...
IT SUITS YOU EVER SO WELL...
ER... WANT TO BUY ANY FISH?
OH YES! WE JUST LOVE FISH! I'LL TAKE A DOZEN, PLEASE.
A DOZEN? WHICH ONES?
ANY YOU LIKE. THEY ALL LOOK DELICIOUS.
YOU KNOW, THAT WOMAN'S REALLY VERY NICE.
YES, BUT I HOPE SHE ISN'T GOING TO FRY THOSE FISH. I CAN'T STAND THE SMELL OF FRYING!
I THINK WE'VE GOT A COUPLE MORE SUPPORTERS!
YOU KNOW, GINA, I'M NOT TOO SURE WHAT WE'VE LET OURSELVES IN FOR... YOU DON'T THINK WE OUGHT TO DROP THE IDEA?
CERTAINLY NOT! AND YOU CAN GO AND BURY THESE TWELVE FISH BEHIND THE HOUSE. I CAN HARDLY BREATHE IN HERE!
RIGHT.
INFLUENZA, DARLING, I THINK THAT GREAT FAT MAN WITH THE MENHIRS HAS A SOFT SPOT FOR YOU... YOU SHOULD HAVE A WORD WITH HIM.
?
19

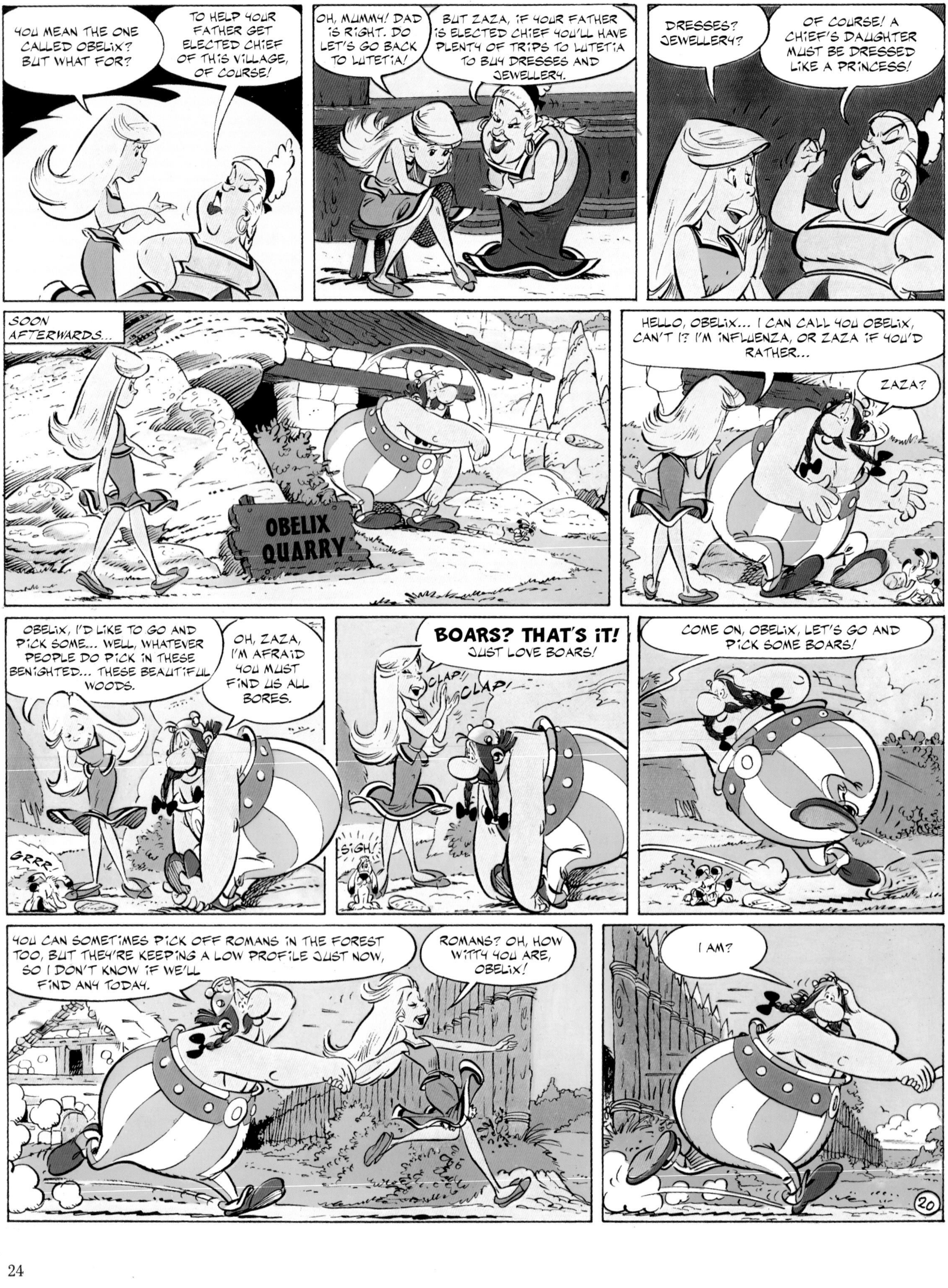
YOU MEAN THE ONE CALLED OBELIX? BUT WHAT FOR?
TO HELP YOUR FATHER GET ELECTED CHIEF OF THIS VILLAGE, OF COURSE!
OH, MUMMY! DAD IS RIGHT. DO LET'S GO BACK TO LUTETIA!
BUT ZAZA, IF YOUR FATHER IS ELECTED CHIEF YOU'LL HAVE PLENTY OF TRIPS TO LUTETIA TO BUY DRESSES AND JEWELLERY.
DRESSES? JEWELLERY?
OF COURSE! A CHIEF'S DAUGHTER MUST BE DRESSED LIKE A PRINCESS!
SOON AFTERWARDS...
OBELIX QUARRY
HELLO, OBELIX... I CAN CALL YOU OBELIX, CAN'T I? I'M INFLUENZA, OR ZAZA IF YOU'D RATHER...
ZAZA?
OBELIX, I'D LIKE TO GO AND PICK SOME... WELL, WHATEVER PEOPLE DO PICK IN THESE BENIGHTED... THESE BEAUTIFUL WOODS.
OH, ZAZA, I'M AFRAID YOU MUST FIND US ALL BORES.
GRRR!
BOARS? THAT'S IT! I JUST LOVE BOARS!
CLAP! CLAP!
SIGH!
COME ON, OBELIX, LET'S GO AND PICK SOME BOARS!
YOU CAN SOMETIMES PICK OFF ROMANS IN THE FOREST TOO, BUT THEY'RE KEEPING A LOW PROFILE JUST NOW, SO I DON'T KNOW IF WE'LL FIND ANY TODAY.
ROMANS? OH, HOW WITTY YOU ARE, OBELIX!
I AM?
20

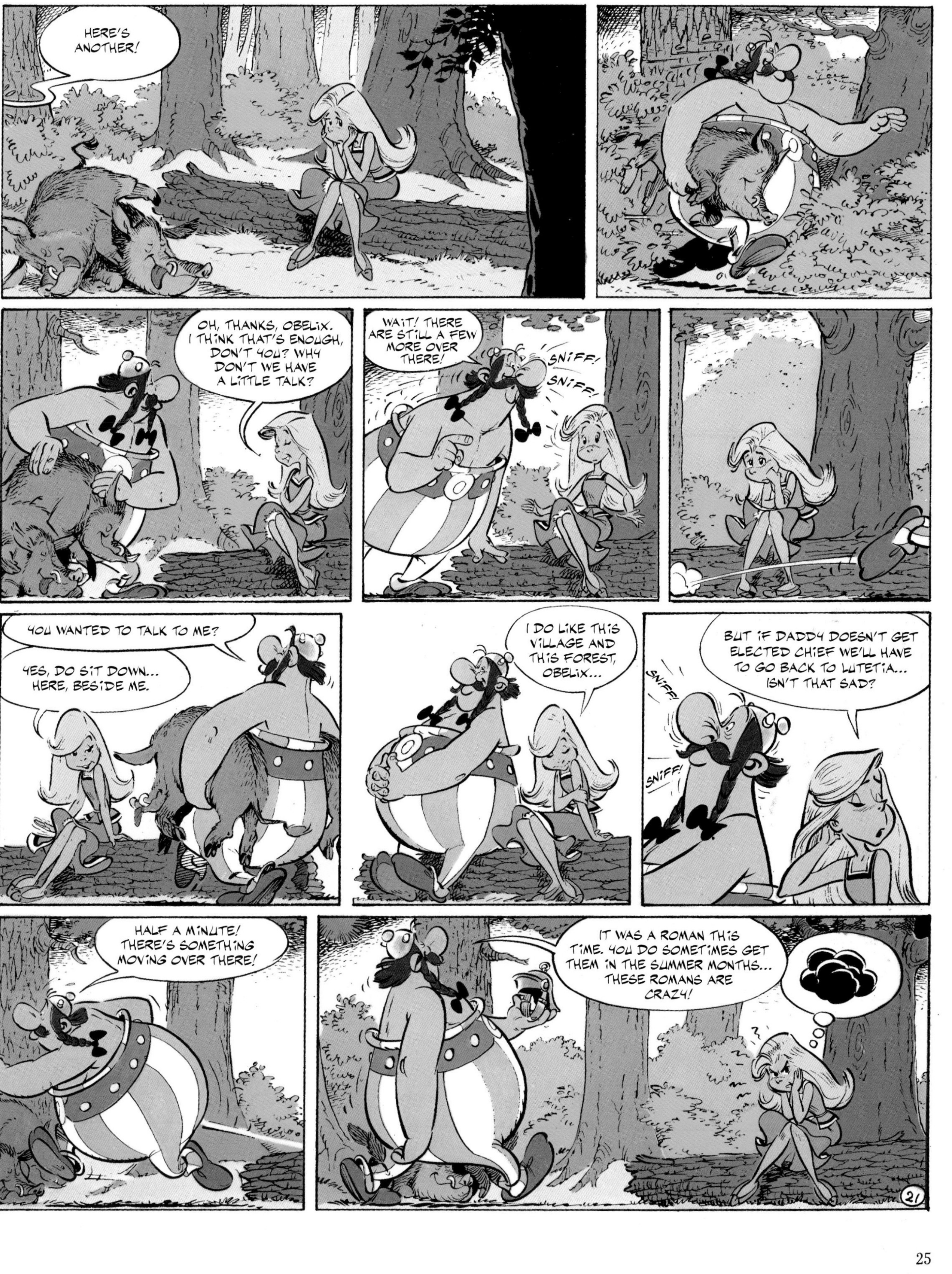
HERE'S ANOTHER!
OH, THANKS, OBELIX. I THINK THAT'S ENOUGH, DON'T YOU? WHY DON'T WE HAVE A LITTLE TALK?
WAIT! THERE ARE STILL A FEW MORE OVER THERE!
SNIFF! SNIFF!
YOU WANTED TO TALK TO ME?
YES, DO SIT DOWN... HERE, BESIDE ME.
I DO LIKE THIS VILLAGE AND THIS FOREST, OBELIX...
SNIFF! SNIFF!
BUT IF DADDY DOESN'T GET ELECTED CHIEF WE'LL HAVE TO GO BACK TO LUTETIA... ISN'T THAT SAD?
HALF A MINUTE! THERE'S SOMETHING MOVING OVER THERE!
IT WAS A ROMAN THIS TIME. YOU DO SOMETIMES GET THEM IN THE SUMMER MONTHS... THESE ROMANS ARE CRAZY!
?
21

WELL, HOW DID IT GO?

OH, HE'S NOT INTERESTED IN ANYTHING EXCEPT BOARS AND ROMANS. BUT I DID TALK TO HIM.

WHAT ABOUT?

YOUR DAUGHTER IS CANVASSING FOR YOU. MEANWHILE, YOU CAN GO AND BURY THAT LOAD OF TROTTERS BEHIND THE HOUSE, AND TAKE THE HELMET TOO!

IF ANYONE EVER DECIDES TO GO DIGGING UP THE PAST BEHIND THIS HOUSE, HE'LL HAVE A FEW ARCHAEOLOGICAL PROBLEMS ON HIS HANDS!

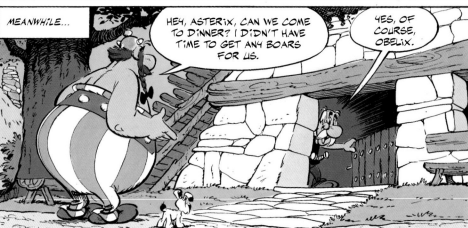

MEANWHILE...

HEY, ASTERIX, CAN WE COME TO DINNER? I DIDN'T HAVE TIME TO GET ANY BOARS FOR US.

YES, OF COURSE, OBELIX.

I'M WORRIED, OBELIX... THERE'S A LOT OF BAD FEELING IN THE VILLAGE. I DO WONDER IF IT MIGHT NOT BE BETTER FOR THE ORTHOPAEDIX FAMILY TO GO...

SCRUNCH! GROUPPE!

WHY?

BECAUSE EVERYONE'S ARGUING, OF COURSE. AND WE MUSTN'T FORGET THAT WE'RE STILL ENTIRELY SURROUNDED BY ROMANS, AND...

WELL, I DISAGREE WITH YOU ENTIRELY!

? ?

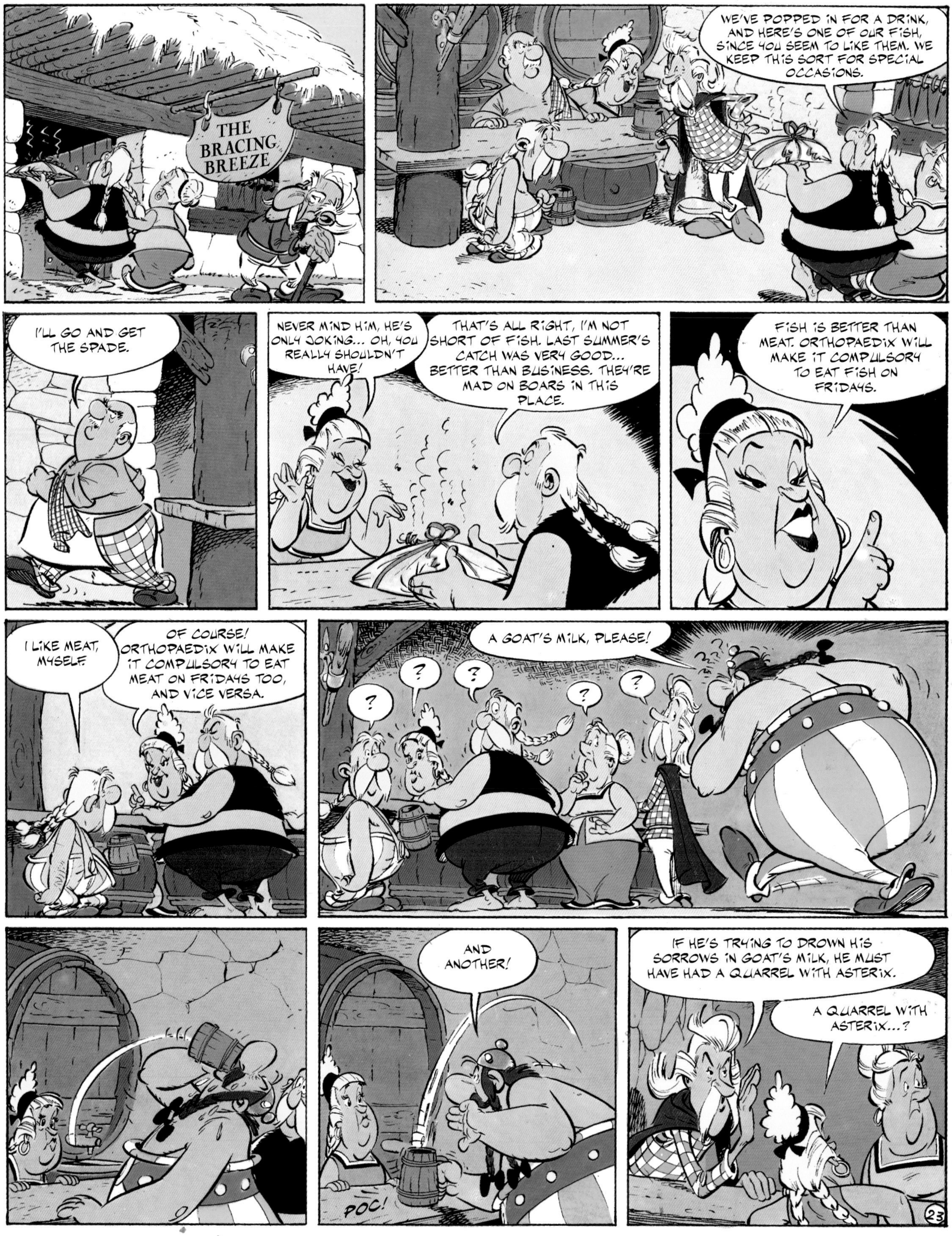
THE BRACING BREEZE
WE'VE POPPED IN FOR A DRINK, AND HERE'S ONE OF OUR FISH, SINCE YOU SEEM TO LIKE THEM. WE KEEP THIS SORT FOR SPECIAL OCCASIONS.
I'LL GO AND GET THE SPADE.
NEVER MIND HIM, HE'S ONLY JOKING... OH, YOU REALLY SHOULDN'T HAVE!
THAT'S ALL RIGHT, I'M NOT SHORT OF FISH. LAST SUMMER'S CATCH WAS VERY GOOD... BETTER THAN BUSINESS. THEY'RE MAD ON BOARS IN THIS PLACE.
FISH IS BETTER THAN MEAT. ORTHOPAEDIX WILL MAKE IT COMPULSORY TO EAT FISH ON FRIDAYS.
I LIKE MEAT, MYSELF.
OF COURSE! ORTHOPAEDIX WILL MAKE IT COMPULSORY TO EAT MEAT ON FRIDAYS TOO, AND VICE VERSA.
A GOAT'S MILK, PLEASE!
?
?
?
?
?
AND ANOTHER!
POC!
IF HE'S TRYING TO DROWN HIS SORROWS IN GOAT'S MILK, HE MUST HAVE HAD A QUARREL WITH ASTERIX.
A QUARREL WITH ASTERIX...?
23

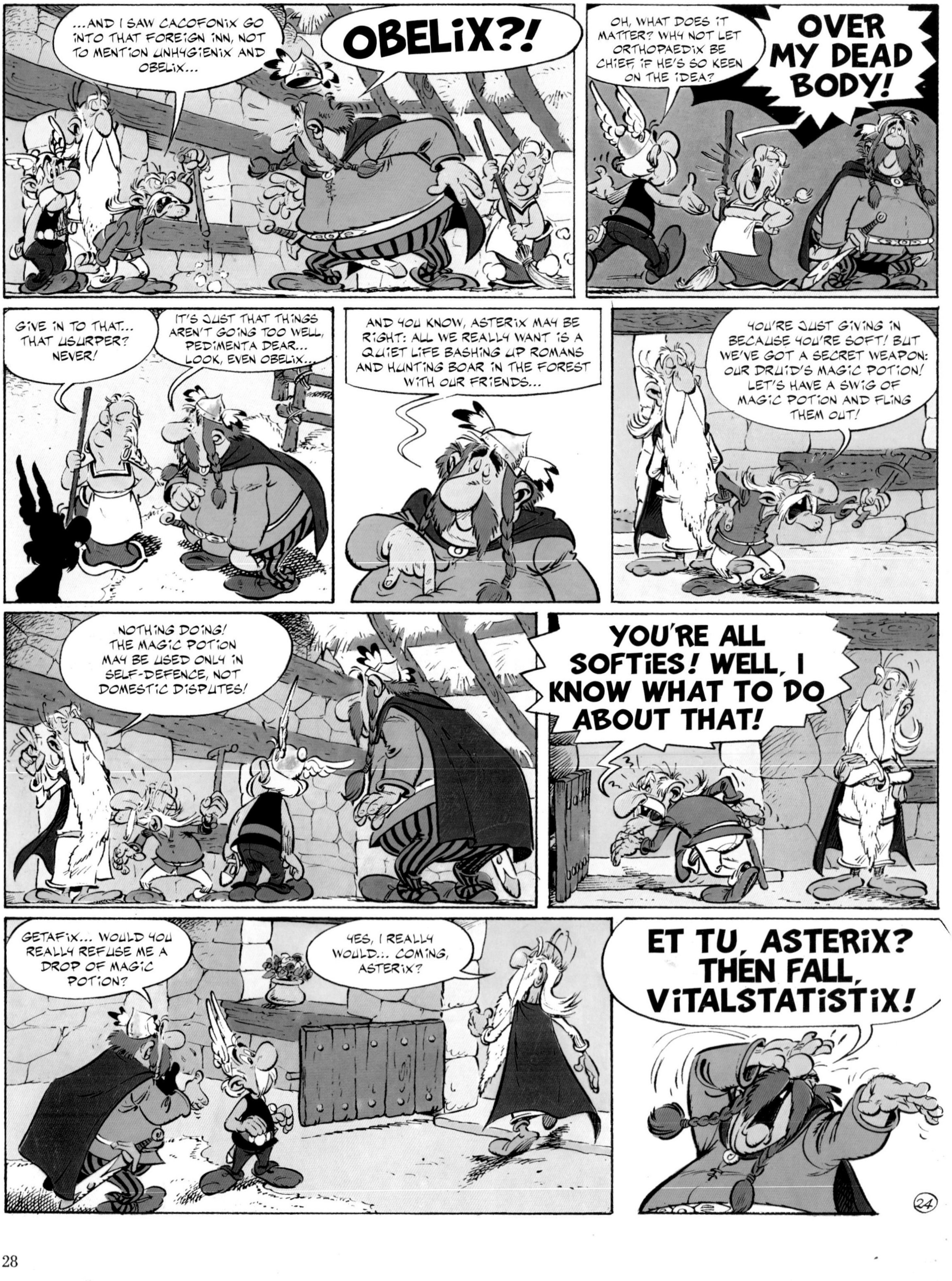
...AND I SAW CACOFONIX GO INTO THAT FOREIGN INN, NOT TO MENTION UNHYGIENIX AND OBELIX...
OBELIX?!
OH, WHAT DOES IT MATTER? WHY NOT LET ORTHOPAEDIX BE CHIEF, IF HE'S SO KEEN ON THE IDEA?
OVER MY DEAD BODY!
GIVE IN TO THAT... THAT USURPER? NEVER!
IT'S JUST THAT THINGS AREN'T GOING TOO WELL, PEDIMENTA DEAR... LOOK, EVEN OBELIX...
AND YOU KNOW, ASTERIX MAY BE RIGHT: ALL WE REALLY WANT IS A QUIET LIFE BASHING UP ROMANS AND HUNTING BOAR IN THE FOREST WITH OUR FRIENDS...
YOU'RE JUST GIVING IN BECAUSE YOU'RE SOFT! BUT WE'VE GOT A SECRET WEAPON: OUR DRUID'S MAGIC POTION! LET'S HAVE A SWIG OF MAGIC POTION AND FLING THEM OUT!
NOTHING DOING! THE MAGIC POTION MAY BE USED ONLY IN SELF-DEFENCE, NOT DOMESTIC DISPUTES!
YOU'RE ALL SOFTIES! WELL, I KNOW WHAT TO DO ABOUT THAT!
GETAFIX... WOULD YOU REALLY REFUSE ME A DROP OF MAGIC POTION?
YES, I REALLY WOULD... COMING, ASTERIX?
ET TU, ASTERIX? THEN FALL, VITALSTATISTIX!
24

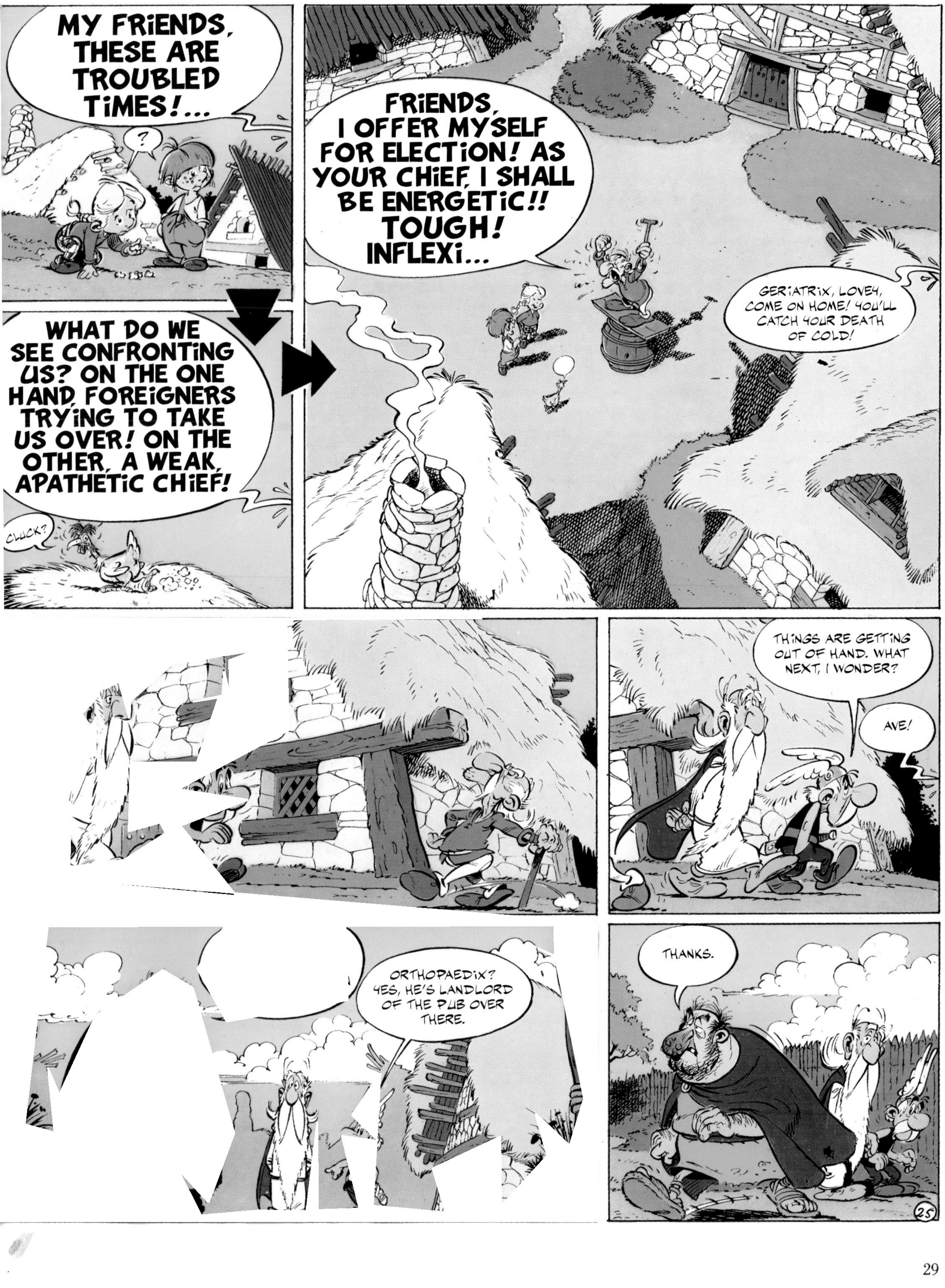
MY FRiENDS, THESE ARE TROUBLED TiMES!...
?
WHAT DO WE SEE CONFRONTiNG US? ON THE ONE HAND, FOREiGNERS TRYiNG TO TAKE US OVER! ON THE OTHER, A WEAK, APATHETiC CHiEF!
CLUCK?
FRiENDS, I OFFER MYSELF FOR ELECTiON! AS YOUR CHiEF, I SHALL BE ENERGETiC!! TOUGH! INFLEXi...
GERiATRiX, LOVEY, COME ON HOME! YOU'LL CATCH YOUR DEATH OF COLD!
THiNGS ARE GETTiNG OUT OF HAND. WHAT NEXT, I WONDER?
AVE!
ORTHOPAEDiX? YES, HE'S LANDLORD OF THE PUB OVER THERE.
THANKS.
25

THE
BRACING
BREEZE

AVE, ALL!

IT'S THE MAN WHO SOLD ME THE VILLAGE!

'SRIGHT. TREMENSDELIRIUS, AT YOUR SERVICE!

WH...WHAT DO YOU WANT?

A DRINK, FOR A START!

WE ONLY HAVE GOAT'S MILK.

BANG!

AH, SO THAT'S WHY YOU LOOK SO GLUM... BUT I CAN CHANGE ALL THAT.

OH? AND HOW, MAY I ASK?

WELL, I HAVEN'T HAD MUCH LUCK SINCE WE LAST MET... I'VE TRIED ALL SORTS OF JOBS... I EVEN SIGNED ON AS A PIRATE, ONLY UNFORTUNATELY THE PIRATE SHIP GOT SUNK...

NOW I WANT MY VILLAGE BACK, CAESAR GAVE IT TO ME!

BUT YOU SOLD IT TO ME!

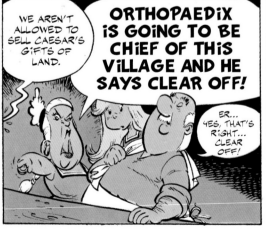

WE AREN'T ALLOWED TO SELL CAESAR'S GIFTS OF LAND.

ORTHOPAEDIX IS GOING TO BE CHIEF OF THIS VILLAGE AND HE SAYS CLEAR OFF!

ER... YES, THAT'S RIGHT... CLEAR OFF!

LOOK HERE, YOU... SEE THIS LITTLE MEMENTO OF MY ARMY SERVICE?

EEEEEK!

26

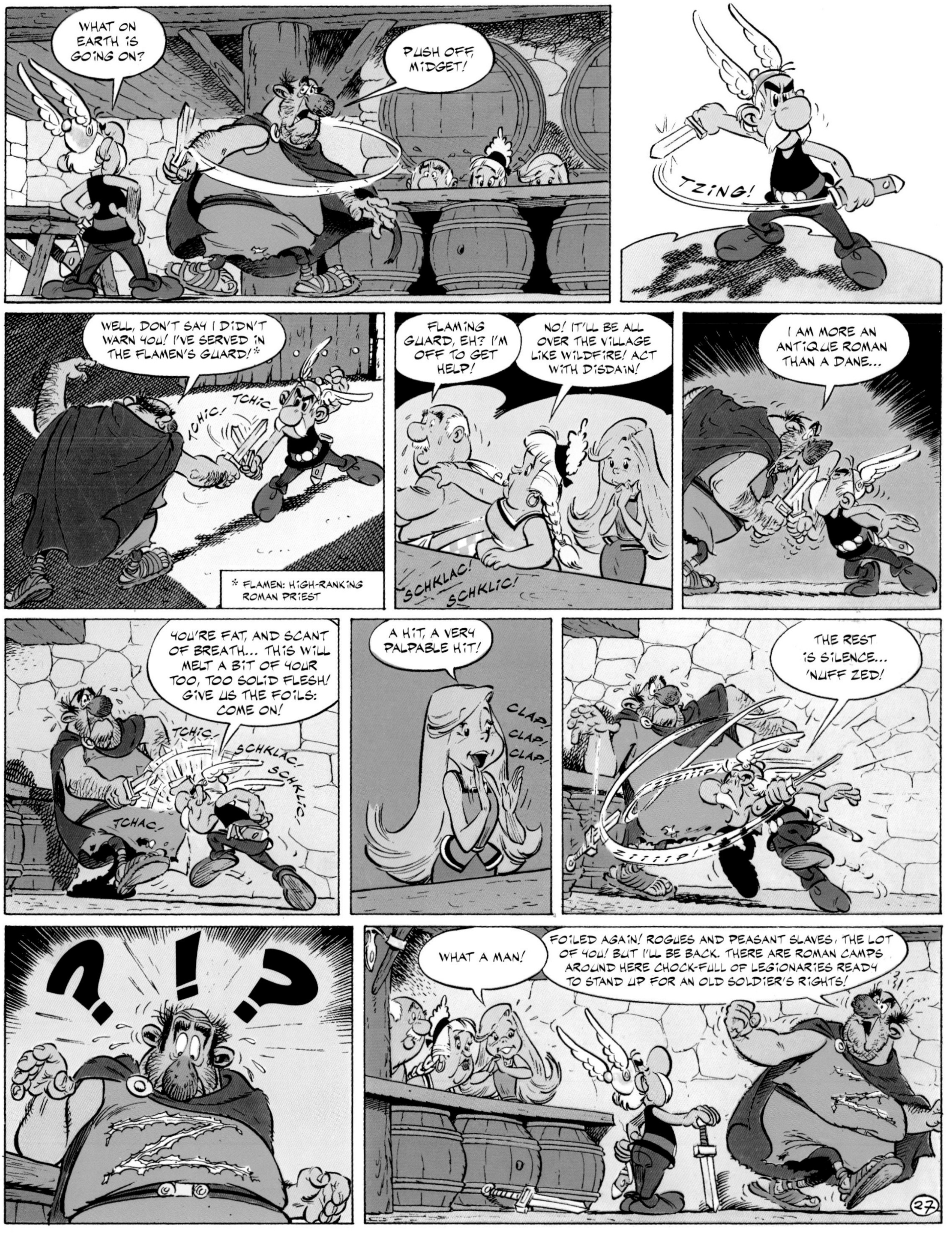
WHAT ON EARTH IS GOING ON?
PUSH OFF, MIDGET!
TZING!
WELL, DON'T SAY I DIDN'T WARN YOU! I'VE SERVED IN THE FLAMEN'S GUARD!*
TCHIC!
TCHIC!
* FLAMEN: HIGH-RANKING ROMAN PRIEST
FLAMING GUARD, EH? I'M OFF TO GET HELP!
NO! IT'LL BE ALL OVER THE VILLAGE LIKE WILDFIRE! ACT WITH DISDAIN!
SCHKLAC!
SCHKLIC!
I AM MORE AN ANTIQUE ROMAN THAN A DANE...
YOU'RE FAT, AND SCANT OF BREATH... THIS WILL MELT A BIT OF YOUR TOO, TOO SOLID FLESH! GIVE US THE FOILS: COME ON!
TCHIC!
SCHKLAC!
SCHKLIC!
TCHAC!
A HIT, A VERY PALPABLE HIT!
CLAP!
CLAP!
CLAP!
THE REST IS SILENCE... 'NUFF ZED!
?!?
WHAT A MAN!
FOILED AGAIN! ROGUES AND PEASANT SLAVES, THE LOT OF YOU! BUT I'LL BE BACK. THERE ARE ROMAN CAMPS AROUND HERE CHOCK-FULL OF LEGIONARIES READY TO STAND UP FOR AN OLD SOLDIER'S RIGHTS!
27

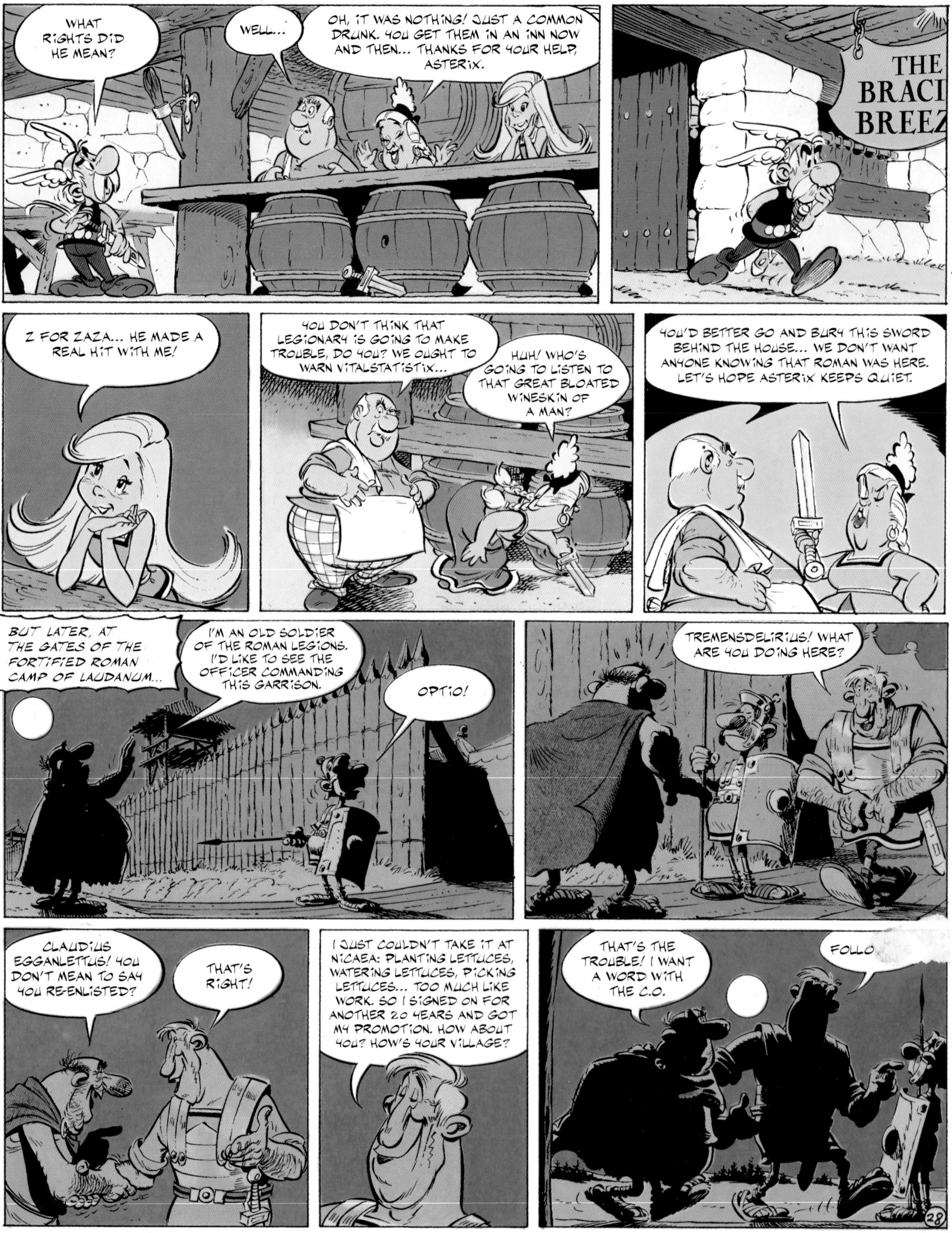
WHAT RIGHTS DID HE MEAN?
WELL...
OH, IT WAS NOTHING! JUST A COMMON DRUNK. YOU GET THEM IN AN INN NOW AND THEN... THANKS FOR YOUR HELP, ASTERIX.
THE BRACI BREEZ
Z FOR ZAZA... HE MADE A REAL HIT WITH ME!
YOU DON'T THINK THAT LEGIONARY IS GOING TO MAKE TROUBLE, DO YOU? WE OUGHT TO WARN VITALSTATISTIX...
HUH! WHO'S GOING TO LISTEN TO THAT GREAT BLOATED WINESKIN OF A MAN?
YOU'D BETTER GO AND BURY THIS SWORD BEHIND THE HOUSE... WE DON'T WANT ANYONE KNOWING THAT ROMAN WAS HERE. LET'S HOPE ASTERIX KEEPS QUIET.
BUT LATER, AT THE GATES OF THE FORTIFIED ROMAN CAMP OF LAUDANUM...
I'M AN OLD SOLDIER OF THE ROMAN LEGIONS. I'D LIKE TO SEE THE OFFICER COMMANDING THIS GARRISON.
OPTIO!
TREMENSDELIRIUS! WHAT ARE YOU DOING HERE?
CLAUDIUS EGGANLETTUS! YOU DON'T MEAN TO SAY YOU RE-ENLISTED?
THAT'S RIGHT!
I JUST COULDN'T TAKE IT AT NICAEA: PLANTING LETTUCES, WATERING LETTUCES, PICKING LETTUCES... TOO MUCH LIKE WORK. SO I SIGNED ON FOR ANOTHER 20 YEARS AND GOT MY PROMOTION. HOW ABOUT YOU? HOW'S YOUR VILLAGE?
THAT'S THE TROUBLE! I WANT A WORD WITH THE C.O.
FOLLO
28

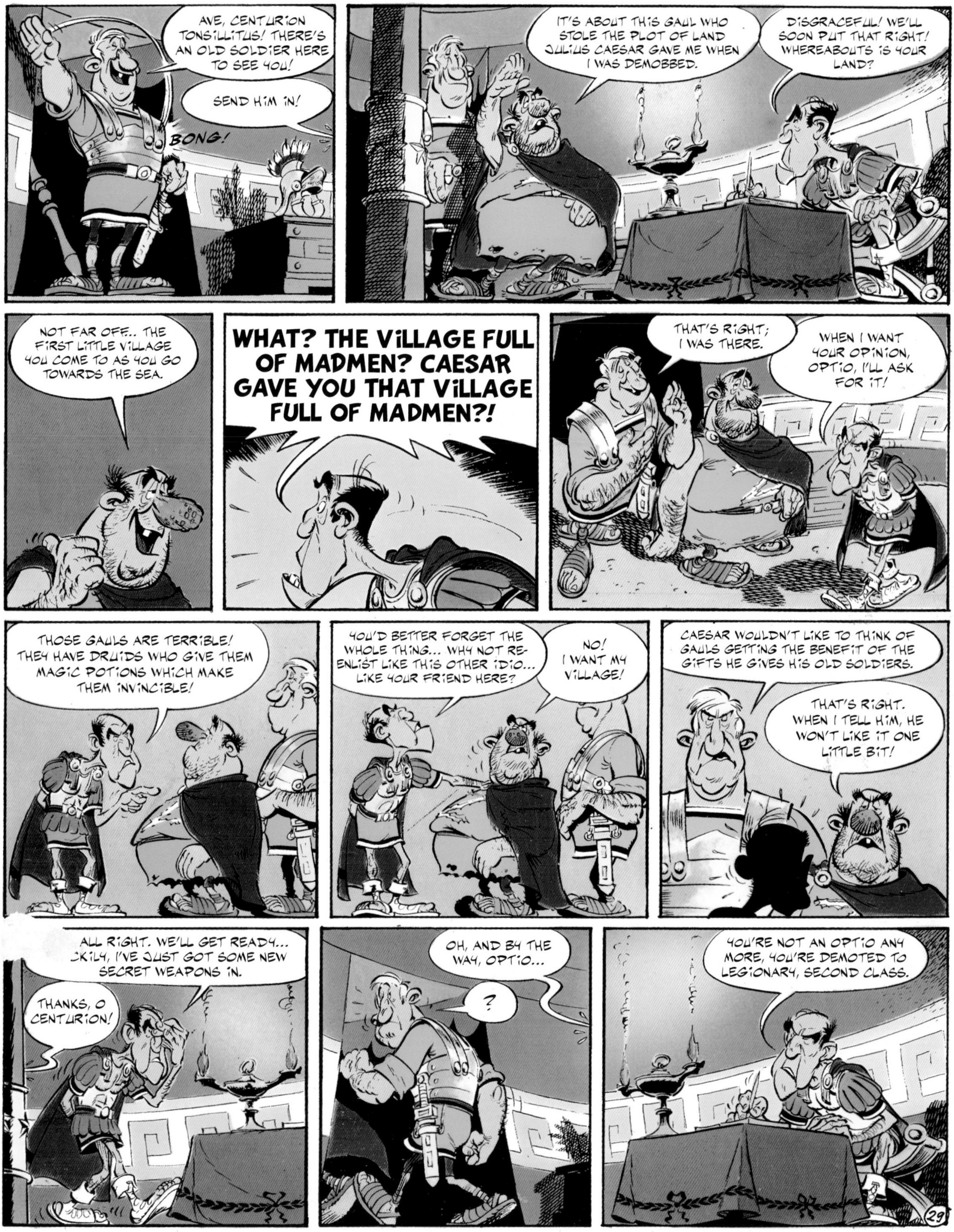
AVE, CENTURION TONSILLITUS! THERE'S AN OLD SOLDIER HERE TO SEE YOU!
SEND HIM IN!
BONG!
IT'S ABOUT THIS GAUL WHO STOLE THE PLOT OF LAND JULIUS CAESAR GAVE ME WHEN I WAS DEMOBBED.
DISGRACEFUL! WE'LL SOON PUT THAT RIGHT! WHEREABOUTS IS YOUR LAND?
NOT FAR OFF.. THE FIRST LITTLE VILLAGE YOU COME TO AS YOU GO TOWARDS THE SEA.
WHAT? THE VILLAGE FULL OF MADMEN? CAESAR GAVE YOU THAT VILLAGE FULL OF MADMEN?!
THAT'S RIGHT; I WAS THERE.
WHEN I WANT YOUR OPINION, OPTIO, I'LL ASK FOR IT!
THOSE GAULS ARE TERRIBLE! THEY HAVE DRUIDS WHO GIVE THEM MAGIC POTIONS WHICH MAKE THEM INVINCIBLE!
YOU'D BETTER FORGET THE WHOLE THING... WHY NOT RE-ENLIST LIKE THIS OTHER IDIO... LIKE YOUR FRIEND HERE?
NO! I WANT MY VILLAGE!
CAESAR WOULDN'T LIKE TO THINK OF GAULS GETTING THE BENEFIT OF THE GIFTS HE GIVES HIS OLD SOLDIERS.
THAT'S RIGHT. WHEN I TELL HIM, HE WON'T LIKE IT ONE LITTLE BIT!
ALL RIGHT. WE'LL GET READY... CKILY, I'VE JUST GOT SOME NEW SECRET WEAPONS IN.
THANKS, O CENTURION!
OH, AND BY THE WAY, OPTIO...
?
YOU'RE NOT AN OPTIO ANY MORE, YOU'RE DEMOTED TO LEGIONARY, SECOND CLASS.
29

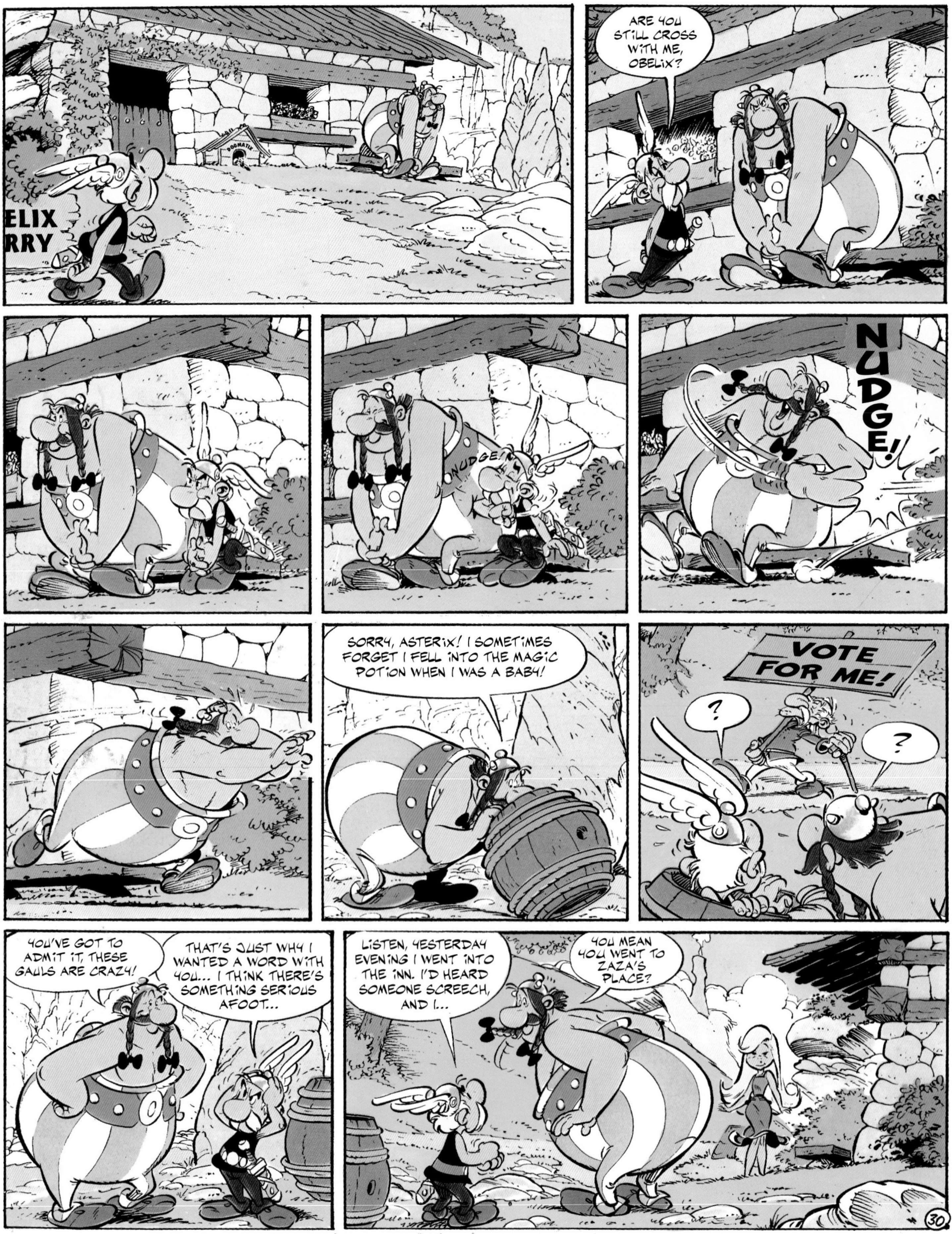
ELIX
RRY
DOGMATIX
ARE YOU STILL CROSS WITH ME, OBELIX?
NUDGE!
NUDGE!
SORRY, ASTERIX! I SOMETIMES FORGET I FELL INTO THE MAGIC POTION WHEN I WAS A BABY!
VOTE FOR ME!
?
?
YOU'VE GOT TO ADMIT IT, THESE GAULS ARE CRAZY!
THAT'S JUST WHY I WANTED A WORD WITH YOU... I THINK THERE'S SOMETHING SERIOUS AFOOT...
LISTEN, YESTERDAY EVENING I WENT INTO THE INN. I'D HEARD SOMEONE SCREECH, AND I...
YOU MEAN YOU WENT TO ZAZA'S PLACE?
30

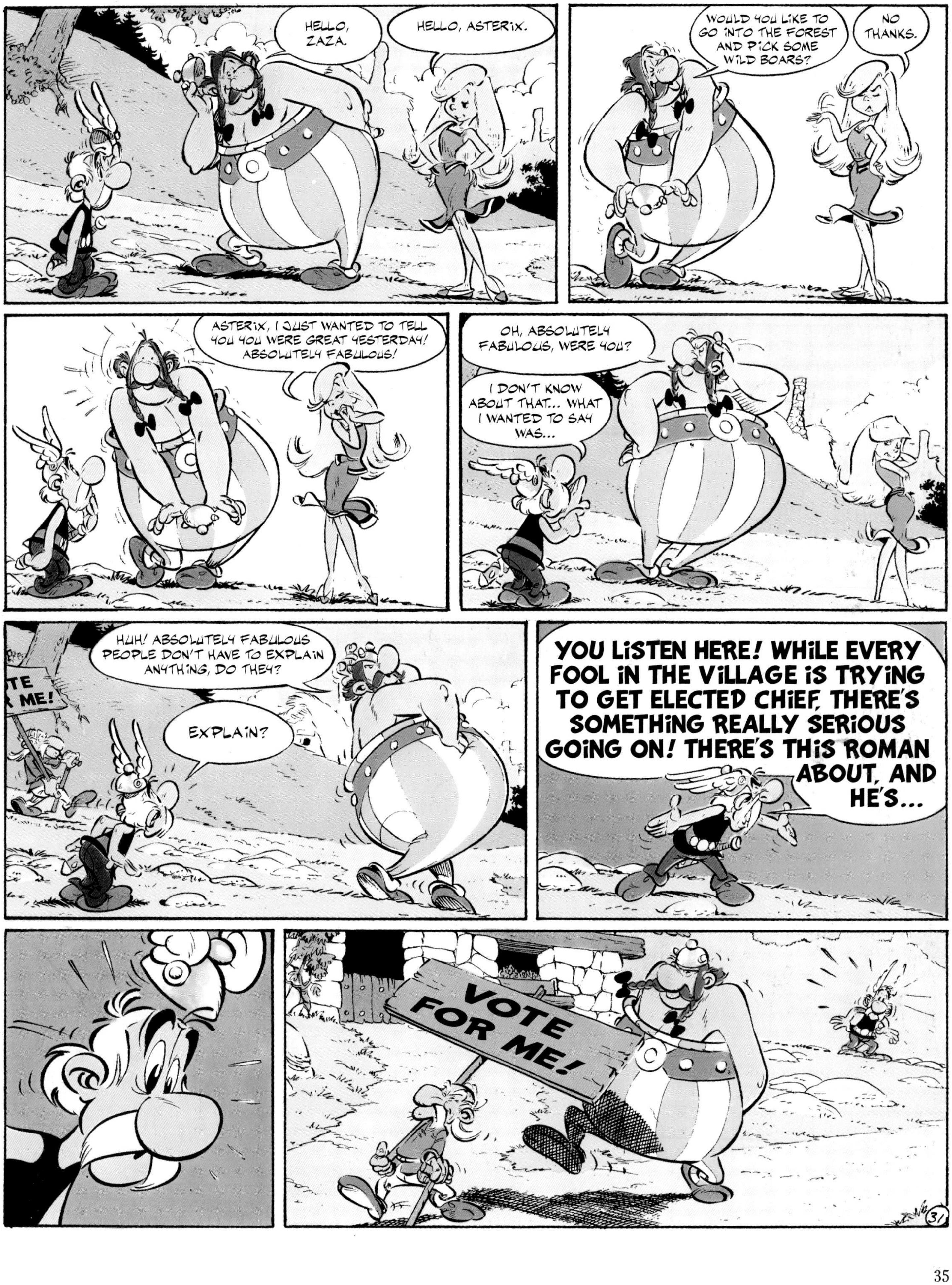
HELLO, ZAZA.
HELLO, ASTERIX.
WOULD YOU LIKE TO GO INTO THE FOREST AND PICK SOME WILD BOARS?
NO THANKS.
ASTERIX, I JUST WANTED TO TELL YOU YOU WERE GREAT YESTERDAY! ABSOLUTELY FABULOUS!
OH, ABSOLUTELY FABULOUS, WERE YOU?
I DON'T KNOW ABOUT THAT... WHAT I WANTED TO SAY WAS...
HUH! ABSOLUTELY FABULOUS PEOPLE DON'T HAVE TO EXPLAIN ANYTHING, DO THEY?
EXPLAIN?
YOU LISTEN HERE! WHILE EVERY FOOL IN THE VILLAGE IS TRYING TO GET ELECTED CHIEF, THERE'S SOMETHING REALLY SERIOUS GOING ON! THERE'S THIS ROMAN ABOUT, AND HE'S...
VOTE FOR ME!
31

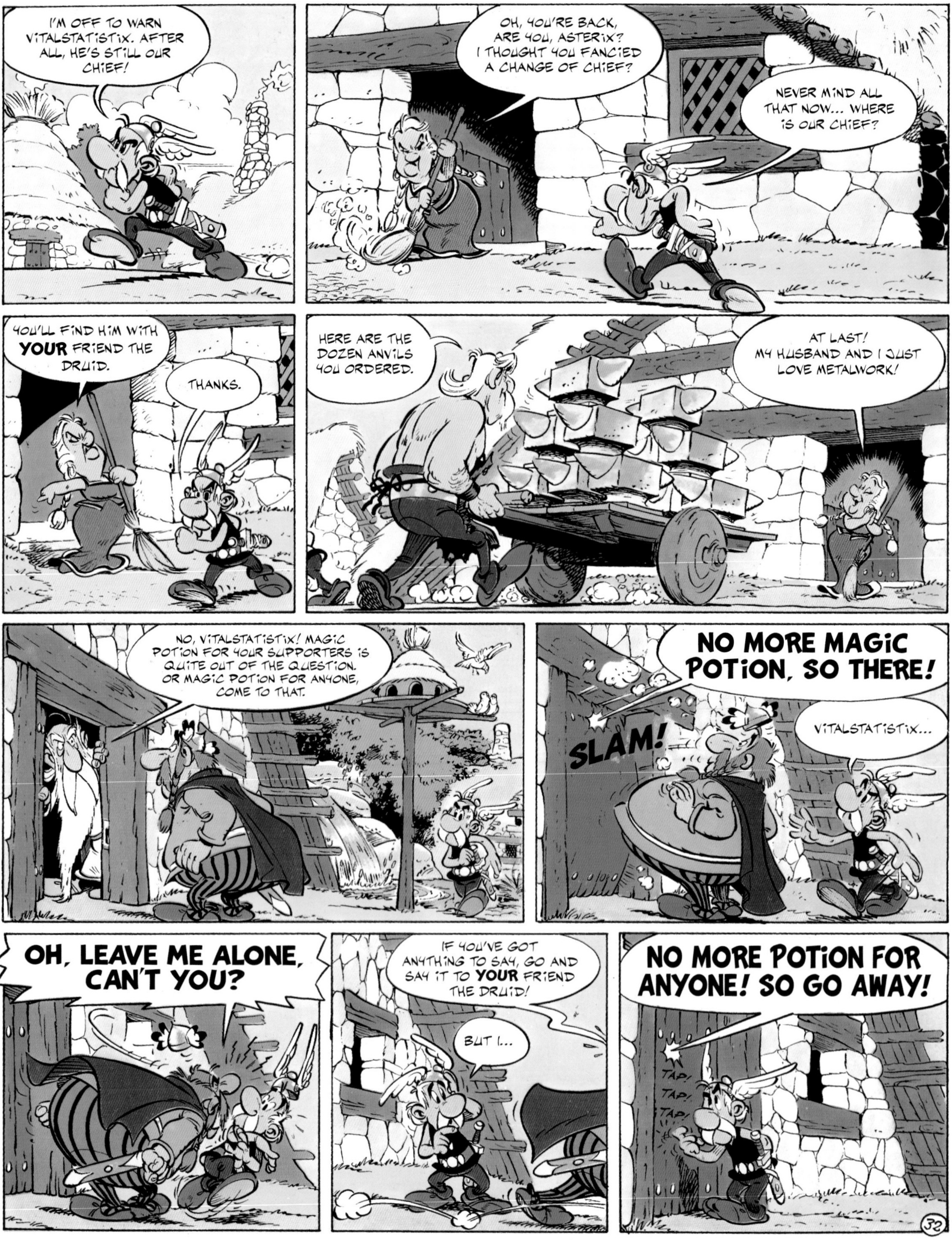
I'M OFF TO WARN VITALSTATISTIX. AFTER ALL, HE'S STILL OUR CHIEF!
OH, YOU'RE BACK, ARE YOU, ASTERIX? I THOUGHT YOU FANCIED A CHANGE OF CHIEF?
NEVER MIND ALL THAT NOW... WHERE IS OUR CHIEF?
YOU'LL FIND HIM WITH YOUR FRIEND THE DRUID.
THANKS.
HERE ARE THE DOZEN ANVILS YOU ORDERED.
AT LAST! MY HUSBAND AND I JUST LOVE METALWORK!
NO, VITALSTATISTIX! MAGIC POTION FOR YOUR SUPPORTERS IS QUITE OUT OF THE QUESTION. OR MAGIC POTION FOR ANYONE, COME TO THAT.
NO MORE MAGIC POTION, SO THERE!
SLAM!
VITALSTATISTIX...
OH, LEAVE ME ALONE, CAN'T YOU?
IF YOU'VE GOT ANYTHING TO SAY, GO AND SAY IT TO YOUR FRIEND THE DRUID!
BUT I...
NO MORE POTION FOR ANYONE! SO GO AWAY!
TAP! TAP! TAP!
32

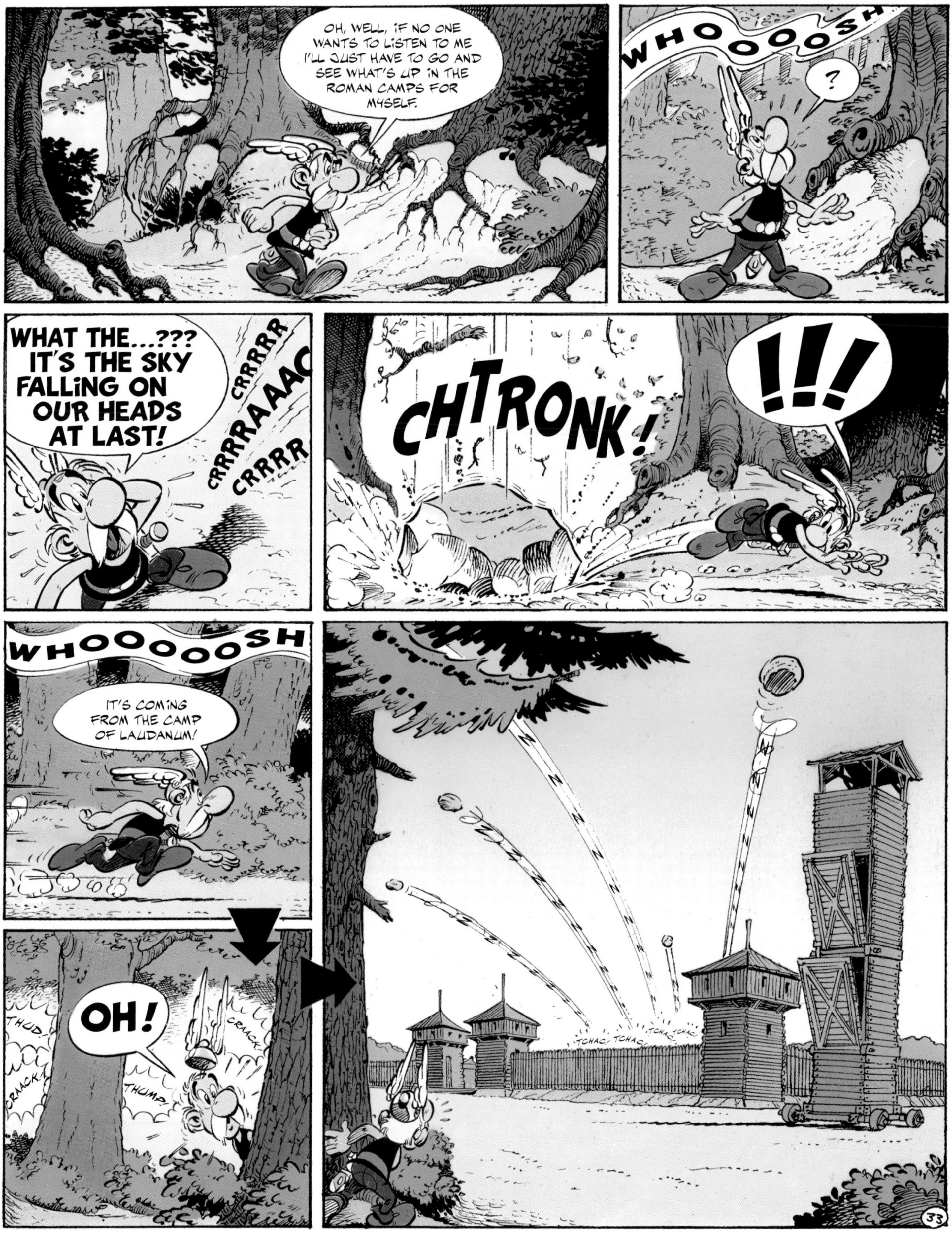
OH, WELL, IF NO ONE WANTS TO LISTEN TO ME I'LL JUST HAVE TO GO AND SEE WHAT'S UP IN THE ROMAN CAMPS FOR MYSELF.
WHOOOOOSH
?
WHAT THE...??? IT'S THE SKY FALLING ON OUR HEADS AT LAST!
CRRRRR
CRRRRAAAC
CRRRR
CHTRONK!
!!!
WHOOOOOOSH
IT'S COMING FROM THE CAMP OF LAUDANUM!
THUD!
CRAACK!
OH!
CRAACK!
THUMP!
TCHAC TCHAC TCHAC TCHAC
33

IF I GO UP TO THE TOP OF THAT TOWER I'LL BE ABLE TO SEE EVERYTHING THAT'S GOING ON IN THE CAMP... LET'S HOPE THE TOWER ISN'T GUARDED!

TWENTY YEARS IN THE ARMY AND I'LL ONLY HAVE BEEN AN OPTIO FOR FOUR DAYS, AND ALL BECAUSE OF YOU! **AND** WE'RE GOING TO GET OURSELVES MASSACRED BY YOUR WRETCHED VILLAGE... MY MATES TOLD ME: IT'S FULL OF DANGEROUS MADMEN!

HUH! THESE NEW WEAPONS WILL MAKE MINCEMEAT OF THEM! A MOBILE ASSAULT TOWER TO BESIEGE THE ENEMY, CATAPULTS, BALISTAS, BATTERING RAMS...

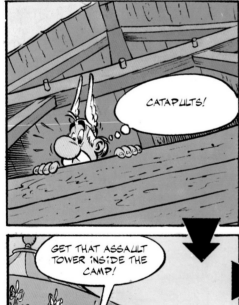

CATAPULTS!

GET THAT ASSAULT TOWER INSIDE THE CAMP!

OH, BY TOUTATIS! AND I HAVEN'T EVEN GOT A SPOT OF MAGIC POTION ON ME!

34

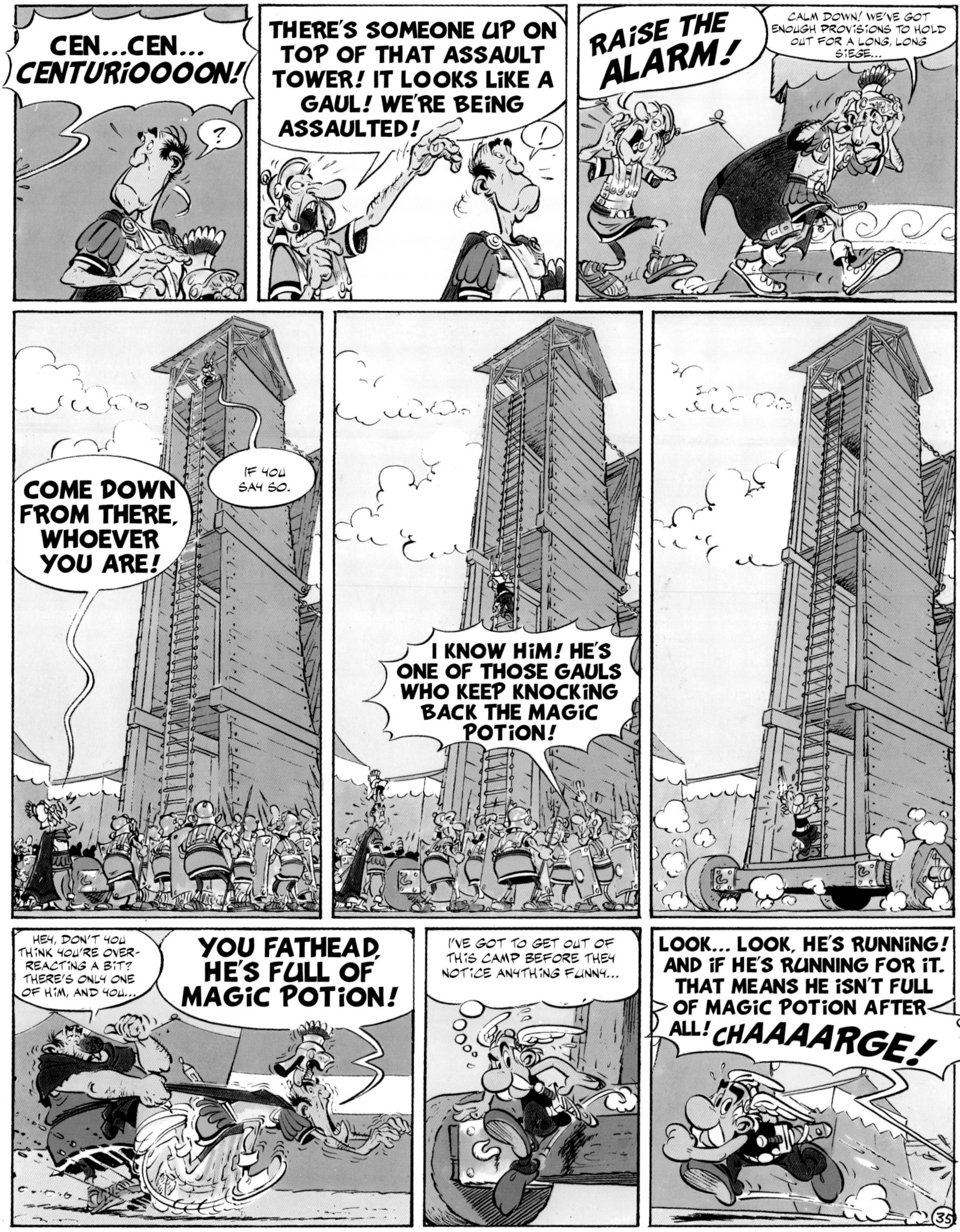

CEN...CEN... CENTURIOOOON!
?
THERE'S SOMEONE UP ON TOP OF THAT ASSAULT TOWER! IT LOOKS LIKE A GAUL! WE'RE BEING ASSAULTED!
!
RAISE THE ALARM!
CALM DOWN! WE'VE GOT ENOUGH PROVISIONS TO HOLD OUT FOR A LONG, LONG SIEGE...
COME DOWN FROM THERE, WHOEVER YOU ARE!
IF YOU SAY SO.
I KNOW HIM! HE'S ONE OF THOSE GAULS WHO KEEP KNOCKING BACK THE MAGIC POTION!
HEY, DON'T YOU THINK YOU'RE OVER-REACTING A BIT? THERE'S ONLY ONE OF HIM, AND YOU...
YOU FATHEAD, HE'S FULL OF MAGIC POTION!
I'VE GOT TO GET OUT OF THIS CAMP BEFORE THEY NOTICE ANYTHING FUNNY...
LOOK... LOOK, HE'S RUNNING! AND IF HE'S RUNNING FOR IT, THAT MEANS HE ISN'T FULL OF MAGIC POTION AFTER ALL! CHAAAARGE!
35

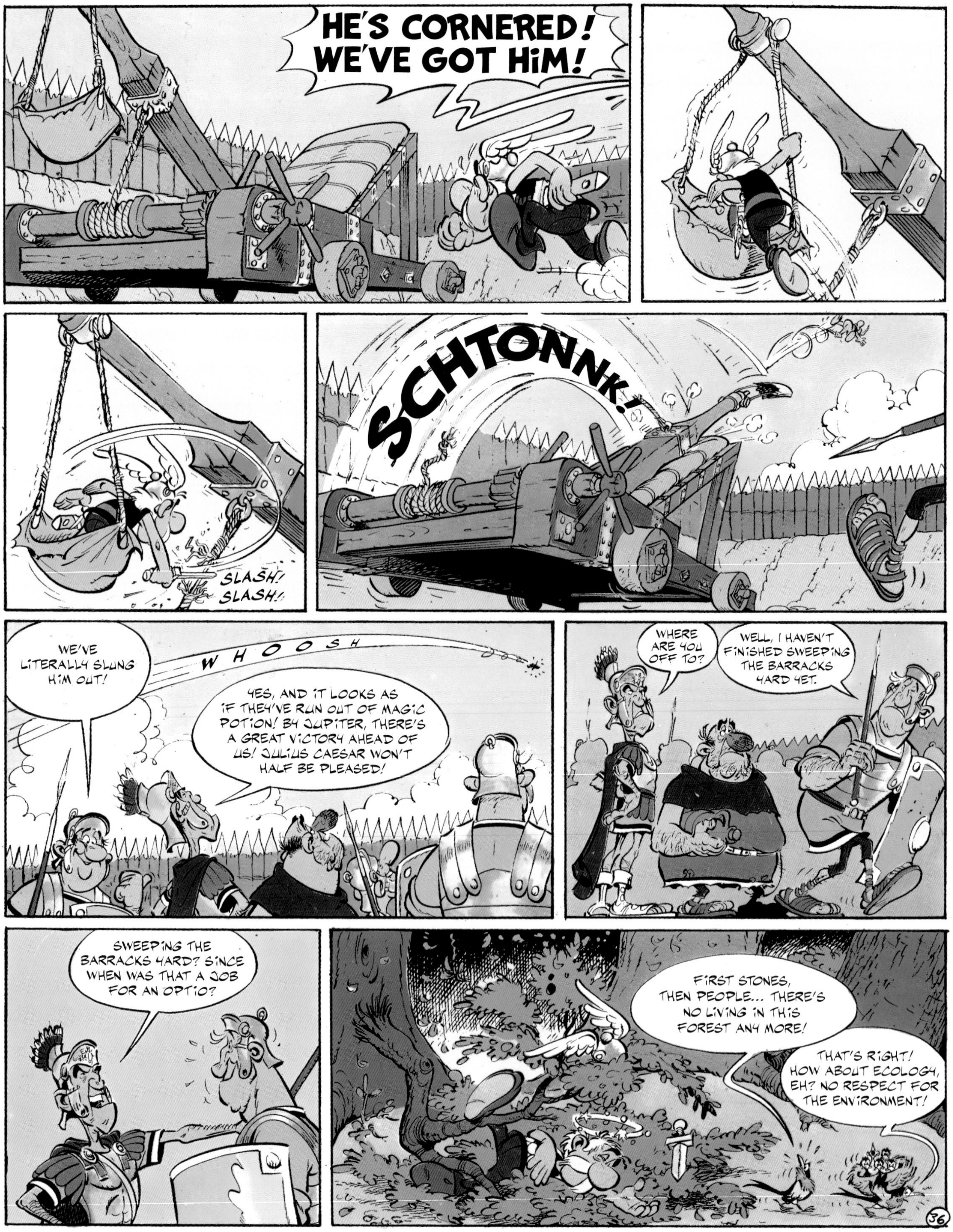
HE'S CORNERED! WE'VE GOT HIM!
SCHTONNK!
SLASH! SLASH!
WE'VE LITERALLY SLUNG HIM OUT!
WHOOSH
YES, AND IT LOOKS AS IF THEY'VE RUN OUT OF MAGIC POTION! BY JUPITER, THERE'S A GREAT VICTORY AHEAD OF US! JULIUS CAESAR WON'T HALF BE PLEASED!
WHERE ARE YOU OFF TO?
WELL, I HAVEN'T FINISHED SWEEPING THE BARRACKS YARD YET.
SWEEPING THE BARRACKS YARD? SINCE WHEN WAS THAT A JOB FOR AN OPTIO?
FIRST STONES, THEN PEOPLE... THERE'S NO LIVING IN THIS FOREST ANY MORE!
THAT'S RIGHT! HOW ABOUT ECOLOGY, EH? NO RESPECT FOR THE ENVIRONMENT!
36

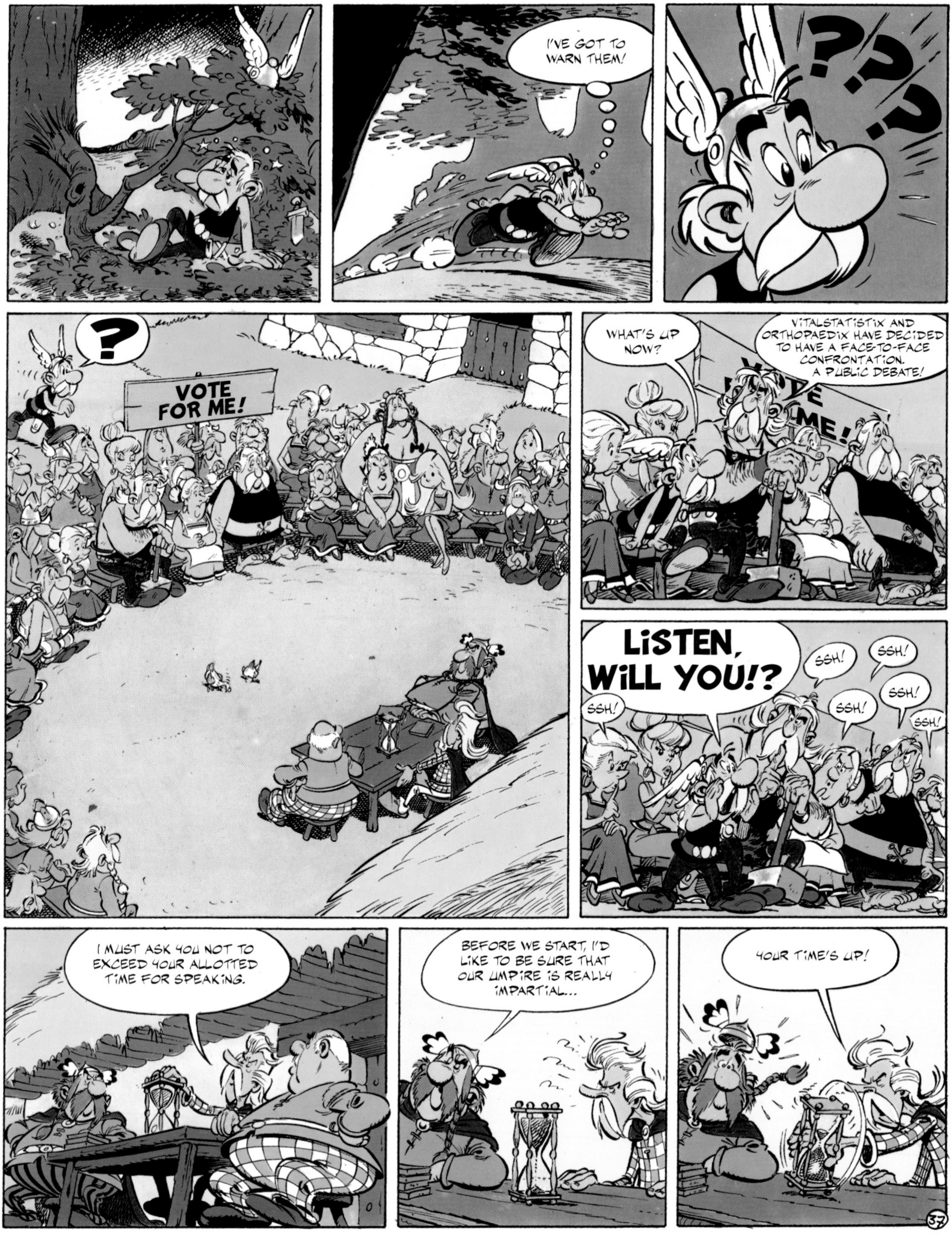
I'VE GOT TO WARN THEM!
???
?
VOTE FOR ME!
WHAT'S UP NOW?
VITALSTATISTIX AND ORTHOPAEDIX HAVE DECIDED TO HAVE A FACE-TO-FACE CONFRONTATION. A PUBLIC DEBATE!
LISTEN, WILL YOU!?
SSH!
SSH!
SSH!
SSH!
SSH!
SSH!
I MUST ASK YOU NOT TO EXCEED YOUR ALLOTTED TIME FOR SPEAKING.
BEFORE WE START, I'D LIKE TO BE SURE THAT OUR UMPIRE IS REALLY IMPARTIAL...
YOUR TIME'S UP!
37

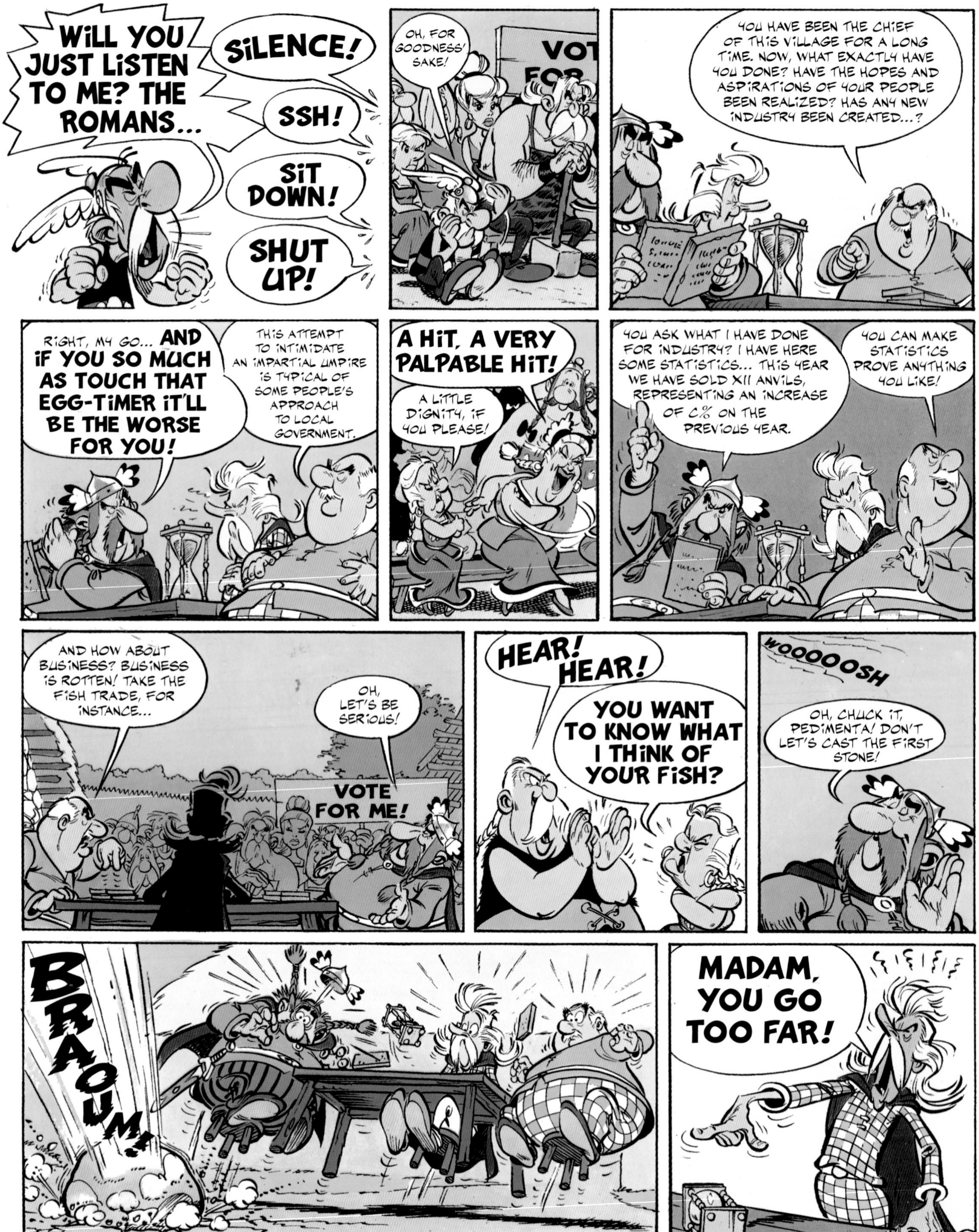
WILL YOU JUST LISTEN TO ME? THE ROMANS...
SILENCE!
SSH!
SIT DOWN!
SHUT UP!
OH, FOR GOODNESS' SAKE!
VOTE FOR
YOU HAVE BEEN THE CHIEF OF THIS VILLAGE FOR A LONG TIME. NOW, WHAT EXACTLY HAVE YOU DONE? HAVE THE HOPES AND ASPIRATIONS OF YOUR PEOPLE BEEN REALIZED? HAS ANY NEW INDUSTRY BEEN CREATED...?
RIGHT, MY GO... AND IF YOU SO MUCH AS TOUCH THAT EGG-TIMER IT'LL BE THE WORSE FOR YOU!
THIS ATTEMPT TO INTIMIDATE AN IMPARTIAL UMPIRE IS TYPICAL OF SOME PEOPLE'S APPROACH TO LOCAL GOVERNMENT.
A HIT, A VERY PALPABLE HIT!
A LITTLE DIGNITY, IF YOU PLEASE!
YOU ASK WHAT I HAVE DONE FOR INDUSTRY? I HAVE HERE SOME STATISTICS... THIS YEAR WE HAVE SOLD XII ANVILS, REPRESENTING AN INCREASE OF C% ON THE PREVIOUS YEAR.
YOU CAN MAKE STATISTICS PROVE ANYTHING YOU LIKE!
AND HOW ABOUT BUSINESS? BUSINESS IS ROTTEN! TAKE THE FISH TRADE, FOR INSTANCE...
OH, LET'S BE SERIOUS!
VOTE FOR ME!
HEAR! HEAR!
YOU WANT TO KNOW WHAT I THINK OF YOUR FISH?
WOOOOOSH
OH, CHUCK IT, PEDIMENTA! DON'T LET'S CAST THE FIRST STONE!
BRAOUM!
MADAM, YOU GO TOO FAR!
38

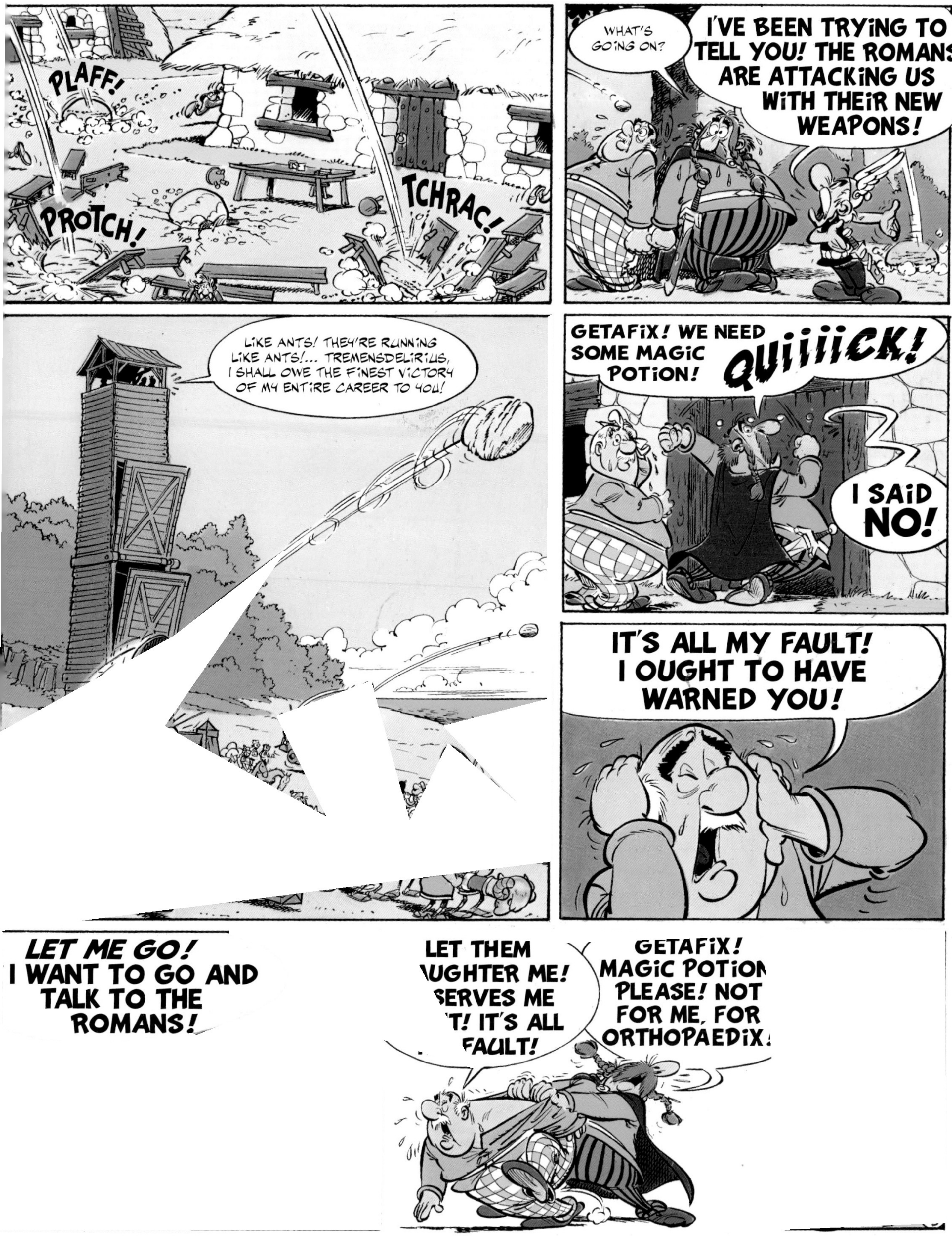
PLAFF!
PROTCH!
TCHRAC!
WHAT'S GOING ON?
I'VE BEEN TRYING TO TELL YOU! THE ROMANS ARE ATTACKING US WITH THEIR NEW WEAPONS!
LIKE ANTS! THEY'RE RUNNING LIKE ANTS!... TREMENSDELIRIUS, I SHALL OWE THE FINEST VICTORY OF MY ENTIRE CAREER TO YOU!
GETAFIX! WE NEED SOME MAGIC POTION!
QUIIIIICK!
I SAID NO!
IT'S ALL MY FAULT! I OUGHT TO HAVE WARNED YOU!
LET ME GO! I WANT TO GO AND TALK TO THE ROMANS!
LET THEM
UGHTER ME!
SERVES ME
T! IT'S ALL
FAULT!
GETAFIX! MAGIC POTION PLEASE! NOT FOR ME, FOR ORTHOPAEDIX!

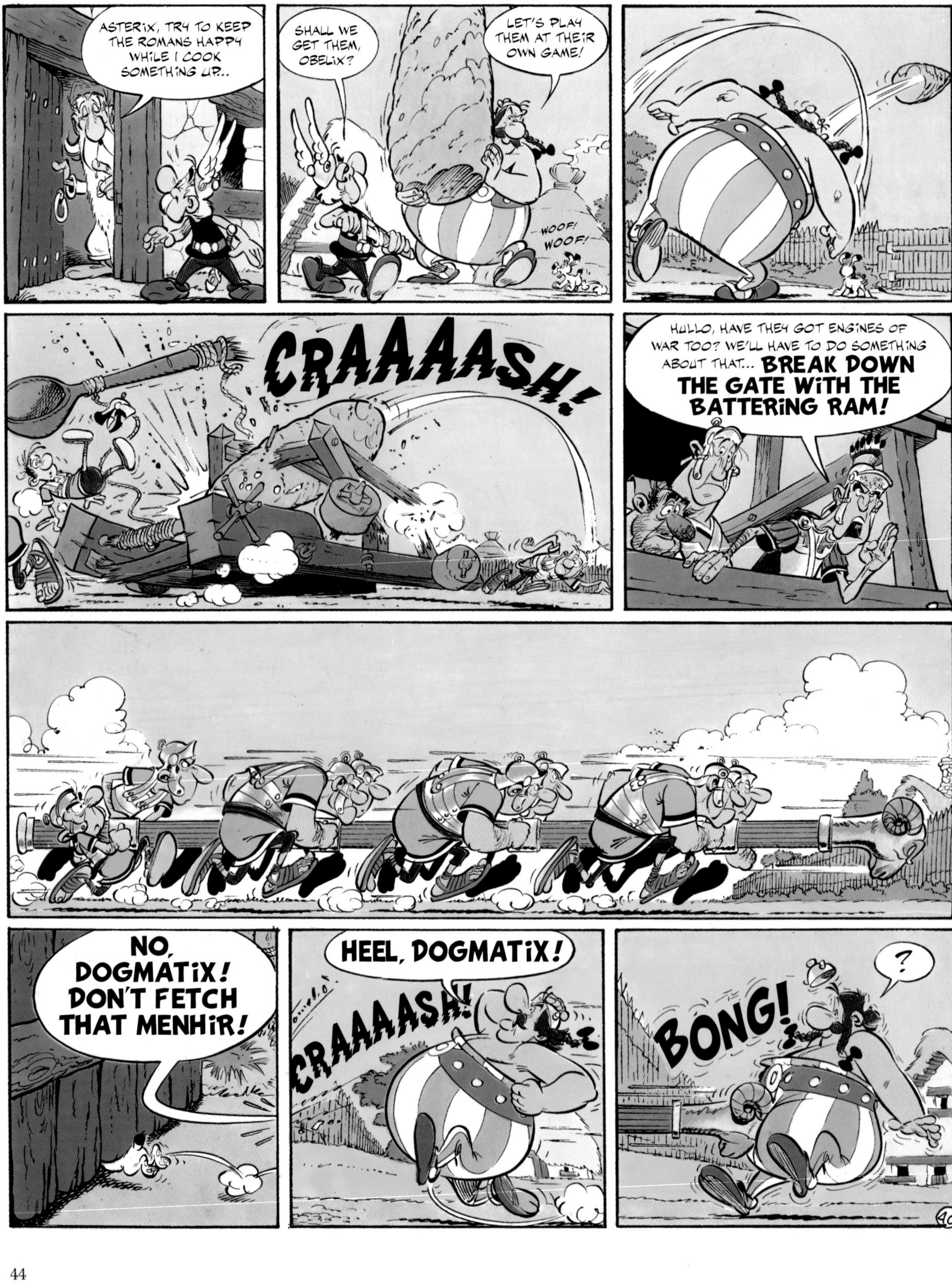

ASTERIX, TRY TO KEEP THE ROMANS HAPPY WHILE I COOK SOMETHING UP...
SHALL WE GET THEM, OBELIX?
LET'S PLAY THEM AT THEIR OWN GAME!
WOOF! WOOF!
CRAAAASH!
HULLO, HAVE THEY GOT ENGINES OF WAR TOO? WE'LL HAVE TO DO SOMETHING ABOUT THAT... BREAK DOWN THE GATE WITH THE BATTERING RAM!
NO, DOGMATIX! DON'T FETCH THAT MENHIR!
HEEL, DOGMATIX!
CRAAAASH!
BONG!
?
40

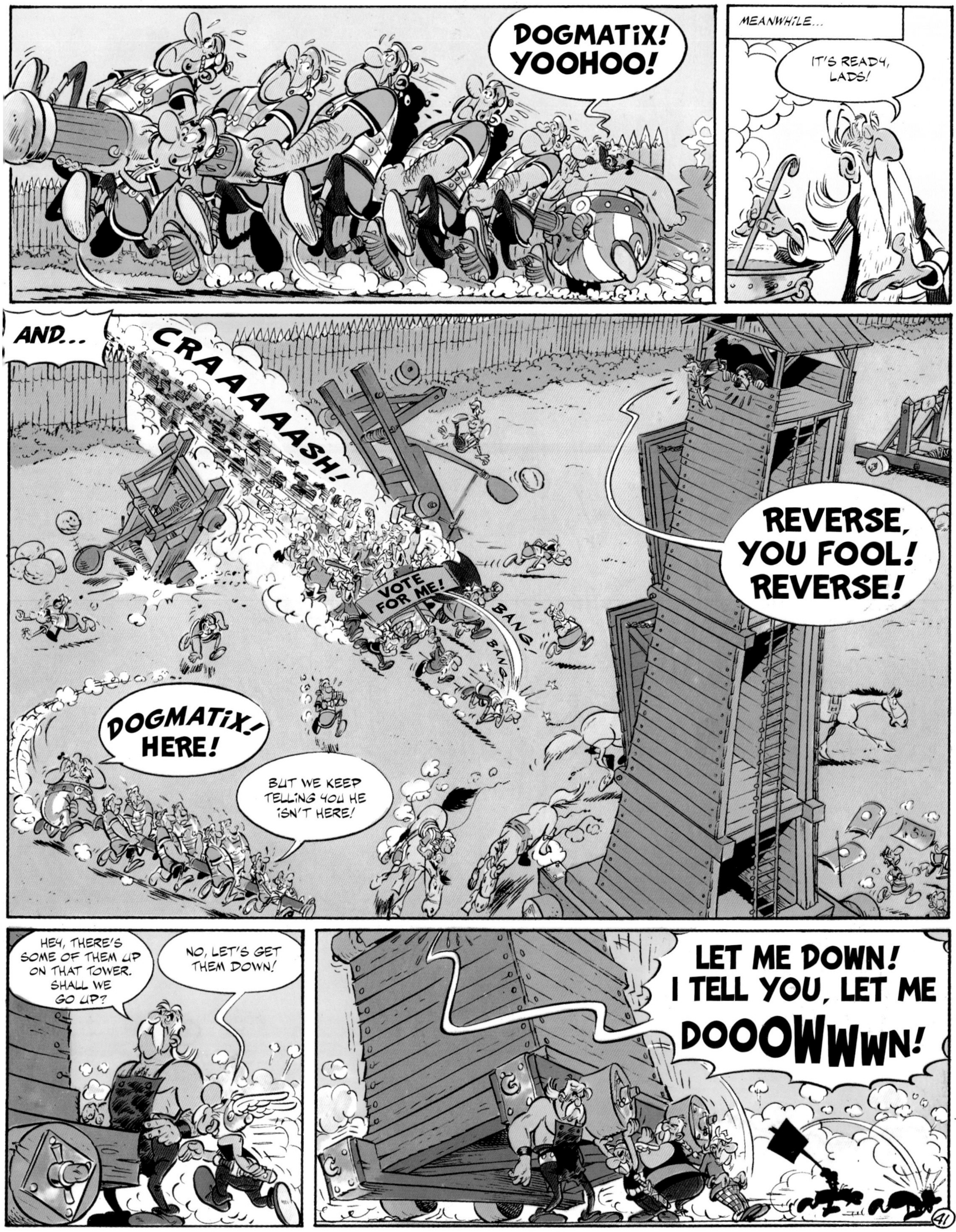
DOGMATiX! YOOHOO!
MEANWHILE...
IT'S READY, LADS!
AND...
CRAAAAAASH!
VOTE FOR ME!
BANG
BANG
REVERSE, YOU FOOL! REVERSE!
DOGMATiX! HERE!
BUT WE KEEP TELLING YOU HE ISN'T HERE!
HEY, THERE'S SOME OF THEM UP ON THAT TOWER. SHALL WE GO UP?
NO, LET'S GET THEM DOWN!
LET ME DOWN! I TELL YOU, LET ME DOOOWWWN!
41

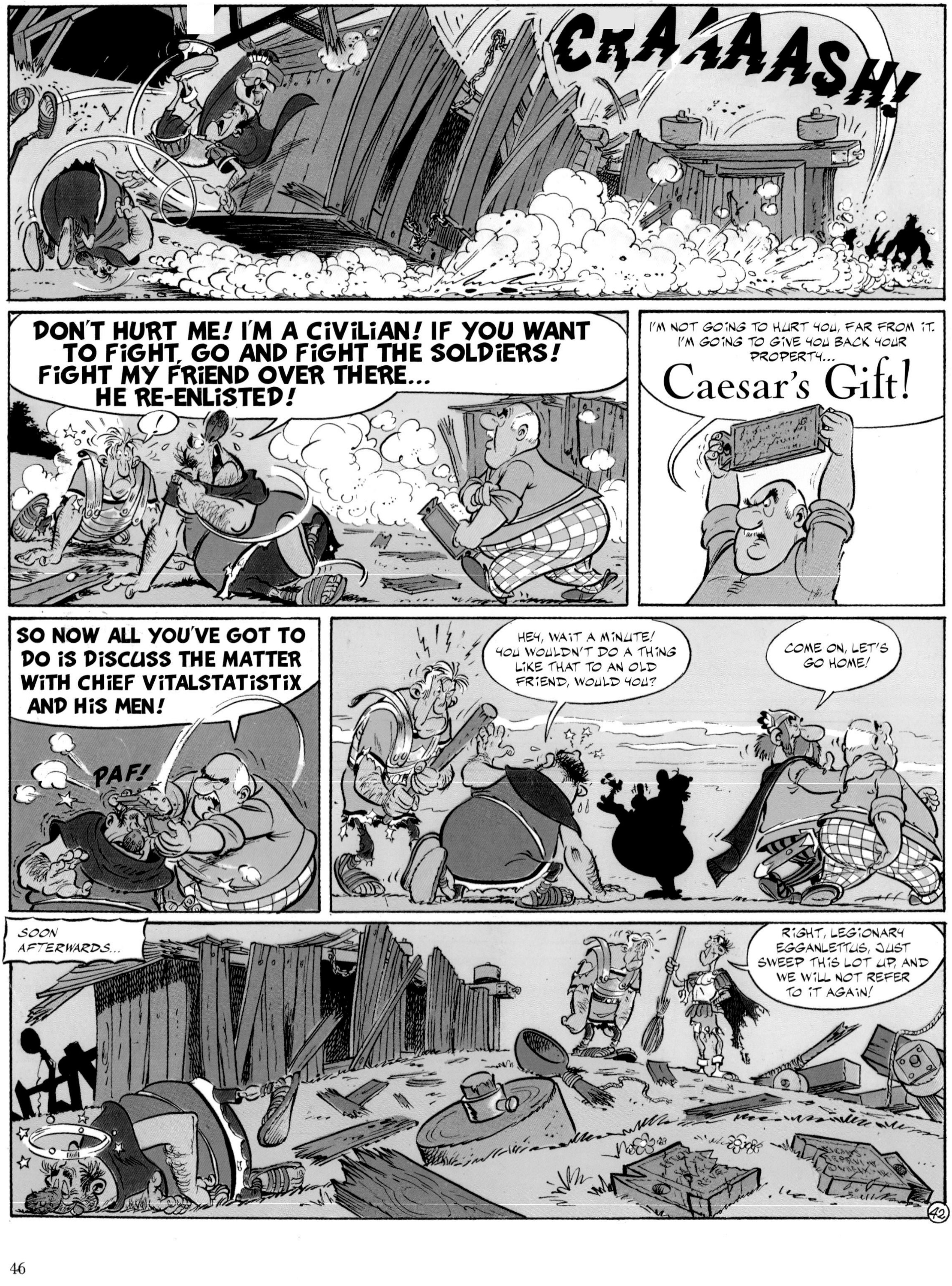
CRAAAASH!
DON'T HURT ME! I'M A CIVILIAN! IF YOU WANT TO FIGHT, GO AND FIGHT THE SOLDIERS! FIGHT MY FRIEND OVER THERE... HE RE-ENLISTED!
!
I'M NOT GOING TO HURT YOU, FAR FROM IT. I'M GOING TO GIVE YOU BACK YOUR PROPERTY...
Caesar's Gift!
SO NOW ALL YOU'VE GOT TO DO IS DISCUSS THE MATTER WITH CHIEF VITALSTATISTIX AND HIS MEN!
PAF!
HEY, WAIT A MINUTE! YOU WOULDN'T DO A THING LIKE THAT TO AN OLD FRIEND, WOULD YOU?
COME ON, LET'S GO HOME!
SOON AFTERWARDS...
RIGHT, LEGIONARY EGGANLETTUS, JUST SWEEP THIS LOT UP, AND WE WILL NOT REFER TO IT AGAIN!
42

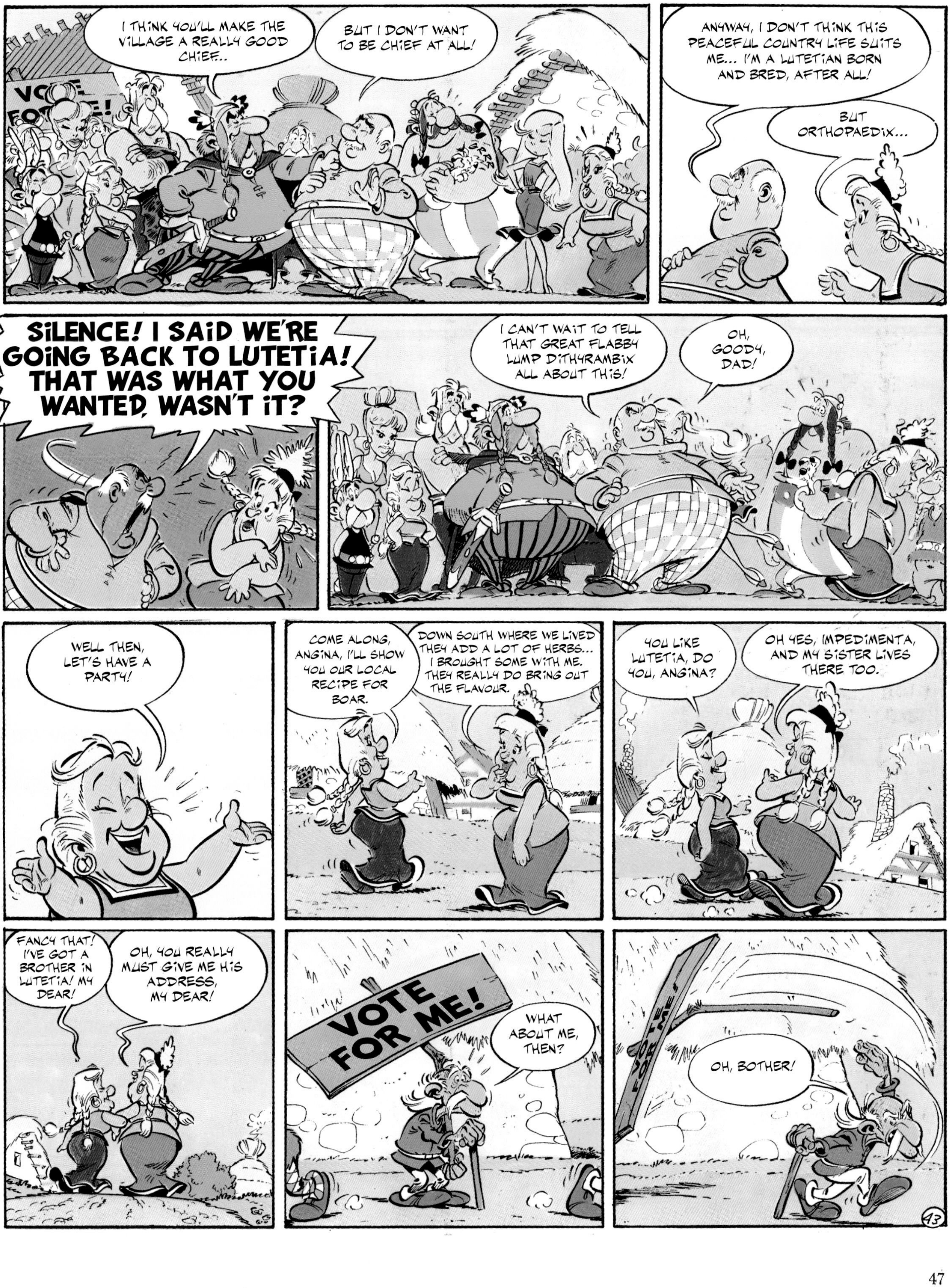
VOTE FOR ME!
I THINK YOU'LL MAKE THE VILLAGE A REALLY GOOD CHIEF...
BUT I DON'T WANT TO BE CHIEF AT ALL!
ANYWAY, I DON'T THINK THIS PEACEFUL COUNTRY LIFE SUITS ME... I'M A LUTETIAN BORN AND BRED, AFTER ALL!
BUT ORTHOPAEDIX...
SILENCE! I SAID WE'RE GOING BACK TO LUTETIA! THAT WAS WHAT YOU WANTED, WASN'T IT?
I CAN'T WAIT TO TELL THAT GREAT FLABBY LUMP DITHYRAMBIX ALL ABOUT THIS!
OH, GOODY, DAD!
WELL THEN, LET'S HAVE A PARTY!
COME ALONG, ANGINA, I'LL SHOW YOU OUR LOCAL RECIPE FOR BOAR.
DOWN SOUTH WHERE WE LIVED THEY ADD A LOT OF HERBS... I BROUGHT SOME WITH ME. THEY REALLY DO BRING OUT THE FLAVOUR.
YOU LIKE LUTETIA, DO YOU, ANGINA?
OH YES, IMPEDIMENTA, AND MY SISTER LIVES THERE TOO.
FANCY THAT! I'VE GOT A BROTHER IN LUTETIA! MY DEAR!
OH, YOU REALLY MUST GIVE ME HIS ADDRESS, MY DEAR!
VOTE FOR ME!
WHAT ABOUT ME, THEN?
VOTE FOR ME!
OH, BOTHER!
13

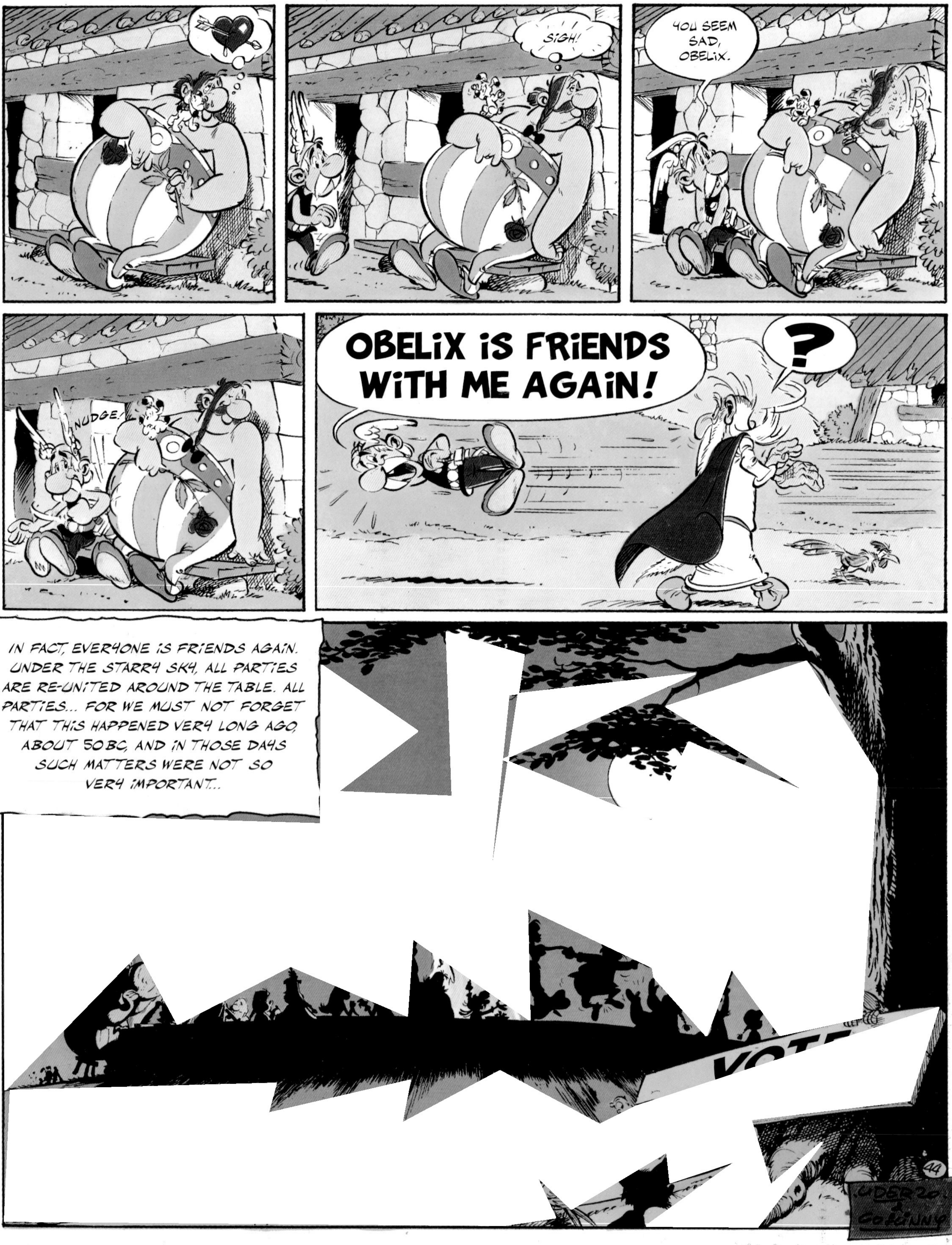
SIGH!
YOU SEEM SAD, OBELIX.
NUDGE!
OBELIX IS FRIENDS WITH ME AGAIN!
?
IN FACT, EVERYONE IS FRIENDS AGAIN. UNDER THE STARRY SKY, ALL PARTIES ARE RE-UNITED AROUND THE TABLE. ALL PARTIES... FOR WE MUST NOT FORGET THAT THIS HAPPENED VERY LONG AGO, ABOUT 50 BC, AND IN THOSE DAYS SUCH MATTERS WERE NOT SO VERY IMPORTANT...
44